Charlcie Arrow & the Magic Red Cape

Charles Beamer

Baker Book House

Grand Rapids, Michigan 49506

To
Charlcie Barr
and our FBC family

Contents

Dirty Dealings

"Get up, get up, get up!" fourteen-year-old Charlcie Arrow yelled in her brother's ear. He mumbled something not very nice, and she shook him by one shoulder. "Get up, I said!" she commanded in her most motherly tone.

Matthew sleepily opened one brown eye. "Aw, leave me alone; it's Saturday." He rolled away from her and pulled the blanket over his tousled brown hair.

She whipped the blanket from the bed and shook the rather stocky ten-year-old again. "Trouble's afoot, and we're needed!"

He sat upright, rubbing both eyes. "What now?"

"Professor Nesbit's missing," Charlcie announced solemnly, shaking long, auburn hair back from her fair face and blue eyes.

Matthew grinned. "He's always missing—like a V-8 engine running on seven cylinders or a skateboard rolling on three wheels."

"You don't understand," Charlcie insisted impatiently. "He's been kidnapped!"

"Oh," Matthew said, suddenly serious. He swung off the far side of the bed, and promptly stepped on a white Arctic wolf sleeping there. "Sorry, Fongo," he mumbled as he stepped over the animal to get his pants and shirt from a chair. Fongo sat up; his head was now level with Matthew's. "What happened?" Matthew asked as he dressed.

"I don't know all the facts yet," Charlcie explained, looking away as her brother dressed. "A few minutes ago Mrs. Nesbit called Mirabelle to ask if Dad was home. She said something about two men walking into Professor Nesbit's seminar in advanced gyrophysics at the university and throwing a sack over his head. Before any of the students could stop them, the two men had rushed the professor out of the building."

Matthew finished buttoning his shirt and patted Fongo on the head. "Did someone call the police?"

Charlcie threw up her hands in frustration. "The police don't believe the witnesses, and they won't do anything! Poor Mrs. Nesbit told Mirabelle the police said the professor is a nut and what can you expect from a nut?"

Matthew frowned. "Sounds like we'd better get over there." Before he could finish Charlcie was out the door.

They ran downstairs, but there, blocking the way, was their stout housekeeper, Mirabelle.

"No!" Mirabelle said, jamming her fists on her large hips.

"We're just going out," Charlcie tried.

"NO!"

"All you ever say is no," Matthew protested. "Just

because Mom died last year and Dad is in Alaska doesn't mean you always have to say—"

"NO!" Mirabelle insisted, moving to block his escape.

Charlcie squeezed around Mirabelle's unguarded side, and as the housekeeper grabbed for her Matthew slipped around the other way. In two jiffies the children were out the front door on a dead run. Mirabelle's voice followed them. "No. No. NO!"

Five minutes later the two were catching their breath in front of an ivy covered stone cottage. They knocked on a round-topped door and a gray-haired lady in a rainbow-flowered dress cautiously opened it. She was dabbing her eyes with a lace handkerchief but she lowered it when she recognized her visitors. "Oh, I'm so glad you came!" she cried. "They . . . they've taken him, and no one will help." She buried her soft round face in the handkerchief, and tears began to stain its lace.

Charlcie and Matthew went to Mrs. Nesbit and hugged her. "We'll help," Charlcie said firmly.

Mrs. Nesbit looked at her, sniffed, and smiled. "Thank you, dear, but what can you do?"

"I don't know exactly," Charlcie replied, hugging Mrs. Nesbit again. "I just know we've got to try to do *something*."

Mrs. Nesbit led them into the cottage, her arms around their shoulders. "If only the professor hadn't always wandered off! Now the police just tell me not to worry; he'll come back in a few days with some other kooky idea he's worked out." She closed the door and sadly faced her visitors. "Only this time he won't be back!" Again she buried her face in the lace handkerchief and sobbed.

"Sit down," Matthew suggested, leading her to what looked like an antique chair.

"No, not that one," Charlcie began.

But she was too late. As Mrs. Nesbit sat down, music started, and bubbles in six colors floated upward as the chair gently rocked back and forth.

Mrs. Nesbit cried harder when she stood to look at the musical chair. "That was the professor's first invention, the Mother-and-child chair. He made it in case . . . in case we ever had children," she sobbed and then collapsed onto the sofa.

Charlcie and Matthew looked at each other. Matthew determinedly whispered, "We're like her children so we've got to do something."

At that moment, a loud clanking noise came from somewhere outside the cottage. The noise was followed by a whooshing sound like a flimsy rocketship taking off.

Charlcie and Matthew rushed out the back door of the house. Mrs. Nesbit followed slowly. Behind the home was a hill almost bare of trees. At the top of the hill was a large barn with huge doors on each end. The doors were open. From them trailed wisps of black smoke which curved up into the sky. There, a flaming tail of a rapidly disappearing rocketship could dimly be seen. Charlcie led Matthew and Mrs. Nesbit up the hill as the tail vanished into the clouds.

"Who, or what, do you suppose that was?" Charlcie asked as she raced to the open barn.

"Martians," Matthew concluded grimly, sprinting

ahead of his sister. "You don't suppose they got . . . IT?"

After reaching the cavernous old barn, they quickly looked around, then plopped sadly onto the floor.

"They got it," Charlcie told Mrs. Nesbit as she entered the barn. Mrs. Nesbit stared at the empty space in her husband's workshop and began sobbing again.

"First the professor," she moaned, shaking her head as she turned to go back down to the cottage, "and now his Truthfall machine."

Matthew grabbed a handful of straw from the floor and threw it in anger. "It's just not fair!"

"That's why the professor was making the machine," Charlcie sighed, looking at the tools and equipment scattered on workbenches and shelves along the sides of the barn, "so life would be fair. Obviously someone wanted very much for him to fail."

"Of course they did!" Matthew snapped. Tears filled his eyes as he remembered where horses once had stood and cows had been milked. What he saw now were empty stalls. Out of one of them protruded the shiny curving bumper and oval grill of a strange, beautiful automobile. "But they didn't get the Responder!" he cried, jumping up.

Charlcie followed him to the stall. They ran hands lovingly over sweeping fenders and a white convertible top. The car's Chinese red paint looked dull in the shadowy stall, but its instruments glistened.

"Say," Matthew whispered excitedly, "maybe we could follow the kidnappers in the Responder!"

Charlcie squinched up her mouth and pushed back

11

her long hair. "I don't think a 1924 Responder could keep up with a rocketship," she cautioned.

"We could try!" Matthew insisted. "Where's the cape?"

His sister looked over the plush leather seats and carpeted floorboards. "It's not here," she concluded, sitting on a running board. "Besides, the professor could make it fly without the cape."

"But we're not the professor."

"He told us not to try to fly it without him," Charlcie reminded her brother. "He said the Responder was quirky and obstinate."

Matthew was not about to be put off. "He just didn't want us to sneak it out and get into trouble. Come on. Let's look for the cape."

They searched high and low, but the red garment wasn't in the barn. Finally they went to the cottage to ask Mrs. Nesbit where the cape might be.

She was calm now. In fact, she seemed more concerned now about the Arrow children than about her husband's kidnapping. "Have some of the professor's Toothlovingsoftdrink and my honey cake," she urged. When she saw they were puzzled by her change in attitude, she smiled. "Have faith. Everything will turn out all right."

The Arrow children were not so sure. They wanted to find the cape so they could pursue the kidnappers, but, so as not to offend Mrs. Nesbit, they accepted pieces of cake and glasses of fruit-flavored soft drink.

"Clues," Matthew mumbled with his mouth full. "That's what we need. Clues."

"Obviously," Charlcie agreed, cutting her cake with

a Knifeforkspoon the professor had invented. "But you don't expect them to magically appear, do you?"

"No," Matthew said thoughtfully. "We'll have to find them." He chewed slowly for a moment, then added, "I wish we had the Truthfall machine to help us."

Charlcie waved her Knifeforkspoon impatiently. "The professor said that wasn't perfected yet. Until it is, we'll have to go on using our own truth-sense, like always."

"Easier said than done," Matthew complained.

"Perhaps," Mrs. Nesbit began, sitting forward on her chair with a hopeful expression, "perhaps the mice can give some clues."

"The mice!" Charlcie cried, jumping up so fast her plate almost fell. Hastily, she and Matthew set the plates and glasses on a nearby table and raced for the old barn.

Charlcie waited to catch her breath. She sniffed the odd mixture of machine odors and hay, and listened to the drip-drip-clunk-clunk of another one of the professor's experiments that still was running. Then Charlcie began to whistle a tune; a merry, springtime, beckoning tune. But nothing happened.

"They're scared," Matthew concluded. "The kidnappers scared them away when they came to get the machine."

Charlcie nodded, then whistled her tune again, more gently. Notes drifted through the cavernous old barn like a fresh breeze, floating into cobwebbed corners and the shadowy hay loft.

"Look," Matthew whispered, pointing to the edge of the loft. "There's one."

13

Charlcie whistled on, concentrating on peaceful thoughts and comforting feelings. One gray, furry head with twitching brown whiskers was soon joined by three others which peered down at the children. Eight bright black eyes now stared at Matthew and Charlcie until the mice were certain that no one would harm them. Then satisfied, the mice scrambled down a spiral ladder to stand in line on the floor of the barn.

From stalls, from under rows of equipment and workbenches, and from hidden holes, other mice appeared. Soon almost fifty gray and brown little animals were gathered in front of Charlcie, listening intently to her tune. Some actually seemed to smile. Most of them swayed back and forth to the music, switching their tails from side to side.

Charlcie stopped whistling and bent down. The mice showed no sign of fear, but she moved cautiously, nevertheless. She looked at the tiny animals until she spotted the professor's favorite—the articulate result of one of his most successful experiments.

"Hello, Padlock," Charlcie said gently.

"Morning," Padlock replied, cleaning his whiskers with quick paws. "Would you please go on whistling? We've not heard the tune for weeks, you know."

"In a moment," Charlcie said. "First, we need something."

Padlock sat up alertly, blinking his tiny bright black eyes. "Anything except cleaning Fongo again."

"Fongo's not here," Charlcie said impatiently, then caught herself and spoke more slowly. "Neither is the professor. He's been kidnapped."

The mice nodded slowly with grave looks at one an-

14

other. Padlock said, "Two men took him and the machine. They took him in a big, flamey-tailed thing that roared and filled the barn with awful-smelling smoke. Did you see it?"

"We got here too late," Charlcie explained. She sat on the floor and crossed her legs. Matthew sat too as the mice came closer. "What else can you tell us about the men?"

"They were big men," Whiskbroom answered. She was another one of the professor's successful experiments, and like Padlock she was very bright. "They were big mean men who didn't say much. They shoved the professor into their flying thing. Can you believe it?"

"I can," Charlcie assured her. She looked at the mice. "Did anybody hear anything that might be useful as a clue?"

"The kidnappers laughed," Whiskbroom said, "but their laughing sounded more like bulls snorting."

A young mouse scampered forward and sat up alertly. "I heard one of the men call the other one Dirk."

"And he called the other one Tirk," Padlock interrupted.

The younger mouse looked annoyed. "You always want to say everything!" he pouted.

Padlock twitched his whiskers and said, "Go on, Lightswitch, if you *really* know something." He snickered as he looked at Whiskbroom and the others.

Lightswitch hung his head. "Just because you were number one on the professor's roll call and I was number fourteen—."

"Please," Charlcie cut in, "we don't have time for squabbling."

Lightswitch raised his head, then whispered confidentially, "I heard the big men say Kalabashar. They said something about how pleased Kalabashar would be if they finally had—."

"No," interrupted another mouse, scooting forward on quick paws, "they were *going* to Kalabashar. It's a place, I think."

"Come on, Doorstop," Padlock said, shaking his head in disapproval, "you were on the other side of the barn when they took the machine apart. How could you—?"

"I heard what I heard!" Doorstop insisted, stamping one of her front feet. "I may not be as smart as you think *you* are, but I heard what I heard. They also said the words *island,* and *oil,* and *billions,* whatever that is." She glared at the other mouse.

Padlock shrugged and looked at Charlcie. "Are those enough clues for you?" he inquired.

"A bit too many," Charlcie murmured thoughtfully, "especially when they don't make much sense."

Padlock blinked at her, tilting his head slightly to one side. "But that's your job!"

"What do you mean?" Charlcie asked.

"Making sense of things is a human's job, not ours," Padlock explained. "We'll help you if we can—like we used to help the professor, after you figure things out."

Charlcie looked at Matthew. He nodded.

"What we figure," Matthew said, "is that we have to follow the kidnappers."

The mice shrank backward. "Follow those men?"

16

Whiskbroom inquired. "Not us. Get Fongo to follow them. He's big and mean like the men. *He* could take them on. We'd only get squashed!" She turned to run.

"Wait!" Charlcie said. "You said you'd help us. You can start by helping us find the red cape."

"You're going to fly the Responder?" Lightswitch asked in amazement.

"We don't have another choice," Charlcie stated, frowning as she looked at the automobile. "We can't follow the men on foot, and we may not have time to try another way before the men—" she sounded uncertain.

"You mean they'll kill the professor?" Whiskbroom asked, sitting up in horror.

"I don't think so," Matthew assured her. "If they were going to do that, they'd already have done it." He glanced at Charlcie. "Most likely they'll try to get the professor to work for them instead of against them."

"Oh," Whiskbroom whispered anxiously, rubbing her whiskers. "You mean they may try to force the professor to—"

"—make the Truthfall machine cover up liars, cheats, and swindlers," Charlcie finished, "instead of exposing them."

The mice and children considered this carefully, then Doorstop ran to Charlcie and sat up. "That would be terrible, wouldn't it?"

Charlcie nodded solemnly.

Doorstop looked at her friends, then at the Arrow children. "We've got to stop Dirk and Tirk, don't we?"

"No one else seems willing to try," Charlcie admitted sadly.

"Well," Doorstop said firmly, "I'll go with you. And I know where the red cape is."

"You do?" Matthew cried, leaping up. The startled mice almost fled, all except Doorstop. She scampered to the side of the barn and stopped in front of a rosewood box that was tucked under a cluttered workbench. The children and mice followed her.

"I saw him put it in here," Doorstop announced proudly.

Charlcie's hands trembled as she bent down and dragged out the box. She opened it carefully.

The mice held their breath and fell backward as a red glow from the box shone onto the floor, workbench, and walls. It became brighter and brighter as Charlcie reached in and pulled out the red cape.

"Oh!" Whiskbroom cried, "it's still alive."

"Of course it is," Matthew said, staring wide-eyed at the cape. "You couldn't suffocate a thing like that."

Charlcie slowly unfolded the large, red cape, and as she held it up, its glow brightened her smiling face. "Now," she whispered, "those bad guys had better watch out!"

"Can we follow them now?" Padlock asked.

"Do you want to come too?" Charlcie asked, folding the cape over her arm.

Padlock hesitated, looking at his companions. Then he sat upright and nodded firmly. "Yes!" he declared. "The professor gave us our freedom, so we've got to do everything we can to free him!"

"It'll be dangerous," Matthew warned.

Padlock, Whiskbroom, Lightswitch, and Doorstop stepped forward to stand in a row like soldiers. Padlock

18

spoke for them all: "Danger or not, we'll do anything we can to help you rescue Professor Nesbit!"

Matthew grinned at Charlcie. "All right! When do we start?"

Charlcie was frowning as she stroked the red cape. "We'll have to pack and get Fongo. Somehow we'll have to outwit Mirabelle."

"Then?" Matthew asked excitedly.

Charlcie looked across the barn to the Responder in its stall. "Then we'll try to fly with the wind."

2

Onto the Trail

The mice went off to pack while Charlcie placed the red cape on the driver's seat of the Responder. Then she and Matthew hurried back to the cottage. "Maybe Mrs. Nesbit knows more," Charlcie suggested. "Maybe she knows more than she thinks she knows."

Matthew nodded as he reached for the back door. He whispered, "Sometimes she remembers things that are important even if they aren't important to her."

They found Mrs. Nesbit humming softly as she washed glasses and cake plates. She wiped her hands while she listened to the children's questions.

"Well now, let me see," she said as she went to her flower-shaped kitchen table. Because she had always liked daisies, the professor had made her a table shaped like a daisy. Her hand stroked the table as she thought. Then her eyes lit up. "General Throckmorton!"

"Who?" Charlcie asked, blinking.

"General Throckmorton," Mrs. Nesbit repeated. She leaned back and folded her plump arms as though she had said everything that needed to be said.

"Who is he?" Matthew persisted.

Mrs. Nesbit sighed. "All I know is that sometimes, late at night, the telephone would ring. The professor would only say, 'Yes, General Throckmorton. No, General Throckmorton.'" She smiled, looking at Matthew and Charlcie.

The children frowned, staring at each other. Charlcie wondered, "Did the general have anything to do with the Truthfall machine?"

"I suppose he did," Mrs. Nesbit answered. "He began calling not long after the professor started working on it." She added, "Brown envelopes from Washington, D.C. started arriving, one each month."

"Now we're getting somewhere," Matthew whispered.

"But not any closer to the kidnappers," Charlcie corrected.

"But we know where to get help to find them," Matthew said. "Come on; we've got to go to Washington, D.C."

"Oh, no," Mrs. Nesbit whispered, shaking her head. "Don't do that! Whatever was going on between my husband and General Throckmorton was very hush-hush. People in Washington might think you're spies if you tell them you know about this top-secret project."

Charlcie stood up. She carefully pushed her chair under the daisy table. "In that case we'll have to be very careful." She glared at Matthew. "Won't we, Matthew?"

"Yes," Matthew replied, stopping himself from running out of the room. "We'll be very careful."

"Good," Mrs. Nesbit said softly as she went with them to the front door. "Because I wouldn't sleep tonight if I thought you children were going to be in any danger. You will be *very* careful, won't you?"

"Yes, ma'am," the Arrow children assured her. Then they headed toward town. Mrs. Nesbit waved to them until they were out of sight.

Halfway home Charlcie stopped in the middle of the road and snapped her fingers. "Awful-smelling smoke!" she exclaimed.

"What?" Matthew asked with a puzzled frown.

"You heard me," Charlcie said impatiently, walking on. "Padlock said the kidnappers' rocketship left a trail of awful-smelling smoke."

"You're not thinking of getting Fongo to track them by smell, are you?" Matthew asked.

"No, no," Charlcie answered with a frown. "We know somebody who has a much keener sniffer than Fongo."

It was Matthew's turn to stop in the middle of the road. "Who?" he asked.

"Mary Bradley," Charlcie said with a grin.

"Blind Mary?" Matthew exploded. "But she's handicapped."

"She's not handicapped!" Charlcie retorted. "She just can't see. Come on. We need her."

Matthew hurried after his sister, spouting objections. "Don't be ridiculous! Mary can't come with us. We can't ask her to put herself in danger, even if her parents do let her go. Besides, just because you feel sorry for her."

"That's enough," Charlcie warned.

"Oh all right," Matthew conceded. "But if we ask her to come, let's ask Brandon too."

"Brandon!" Charlcie snapped. "What good is that smart-aleck?"

"I don't like him much either, but you have to admit he's awfully smart. You just think he's a smart-aleck because he knows the answers to questions that stump you."

Charlcie grumbled, "If we took him he'd fill the Responder with his stupid books."

"You've always told me that books weren't stupid." Matthew grinned.

Charlcie ignored this. "Brandon-dear's mommy probably wouldn't let him go, anyway. She hardly lets him go to the swimming pool where there are at least six lifeguards. There aren't *any* lifeguards where we're going."

Matthew sniffed. "You're just jealous because he's younger but smarter than you."

"Jealous? Me?" Charlcie cried. Then she sighed. "Okay, I'll make a deal with you. I'll ask Mary and you can ask Brandon-dear."

Matthew nodded. "Shall we ask them now?"

"Let's pack first."

Mirabelle followed them around the house. She said, "No!" when Matthew stuffed his clothes into a suitcase. She said, "No!" when Charlcie tucked dresses, jeans, sunsuits, and blouses into her tan suitcase. Then Mirabelle said, "No!" when the children packed a sack lunch.

"Don't forget Fongo's dog food," Matthew reminded his sister.

Charlcie packed the dog chow, then sat on her suitcase to close it. At last she returned to the kitchen to write a letter for their father in case they didn't return. She addressed it, "Mr. John Arrow, Shell Petroleum Exploration Expedition, c/o Anchorage, Alaska." She told Mirabelle what to do with the letter and laid it on her lap.

"NO!" Mirabelle yelped, covering her face with her hands. She refused to touch the letter.

Charlcie picked up her suitcase and said softly to the sobbing housekeeper, "We'll be all right, Mirabelle. We won't get in trouble. I promise."

"No-o-o," Mirabelle wailed.

"Sorry, Mirabelle," Charlcie said, glancing at Matthew and Fongo. "We've got to do what we've got to do." She kissed the housekeeper and hurried with the others out the front door.

From behind them came a mournful, "NO-OO-OOO!"

"Poor Mirabelle," Charlcie muttered shaking her head as they headed down the street toward Mary Bradley's home.

Mary was scheduled that very day to go to a special camp in the mountains for two weeks. It took Charlcie and Matthew only ten minutes to persuade the Bradleys they could take Mary to the airport. Since Mary was already packed, the trio of children were on their way in a jiffy.

"Mr. and Mrs. Bradley sure trust us," Charlcie observed grimly to her brother as they hurried across town toward Brandon's home.

Matthew chewed on his lip and looked at Mary, who was holding Charlcie's hand. "I don't know about this," Matthew sighed. "What would happen if—"

"Don't worry about it," Mary piped up cheerfully. "Going on an adventure with you will be lots more fun than camp. I'll be safe."

Charlcie and Matthew anxiously looked at each other.

"But I don't really understand what's happening," Mary began, looking directly at Charlcie.

They told her what had happened. When they finished, Mary was frowning.

"Are you sure you want me to come with you?" was her only question.

"Yes," Charlcie said emphatically, squeezing Mary's hand. "I honestly don't know anyone who can decipher smells and sounds better than you. A lot of what we'll have to do will be like spying. You know, creeping around in the dark and following the smell of rocketships—things like that."

"Oh," Mary murmured softly, slowing down.

"You're not afraid, are you?" Matthew asked, looking concerned.

"No," Mary said, tilting her head. "I know you won't let me get hurt. I know Fongo's with us too. He's strong and a very good guardian. But—"

"What?" Charlcie asked breathlessly.

Mary shrugged, then lifted her suitcase. "I just realized how much danger the professor is in. This is serious, isn't it?"

"It's not like going to camp," Charlcie admitted, arching one eyebrow at Matthew.

Getting Brandon Arnold Brenson, III, sprung from his house was a lot more difficult than enlisting Mary. For him the Arrow children had to find a new technique altogether. Matthew called Brandon from a pay telephone.

While they waited on a street corner, Brandon packed and slipped out his bedroom window. He came hobbling toward them, bent over from the weight of a large suitcase.

"See," Charlcie grumbled to Matthew before Brandon reached them, "I told you he'd bring a whole library."

"Hello, Charlcie, Matthew, Mary," Brandon said. He set his suitcase on the sidewalk with a thump. "What's up?" he asked, wiping sweat from his pale face. He removed his glasses, cleaned them, then smoothed down his thin blond hair while Charlcie and Matthew stared at him.

"I told you," Matthew replied. "Professor Nesbit's been kidnapped."

Brandon's expression clouded as he rubbed his chin. "You said the kidnappers took him away in a rocket-ship?" he asked, peering owlishly at Matthew.

Matthew nodded.

"Then this is clearly a matter for the FBI," Brandon announced, folding his thin arms. "Interstate kidnappings are always turned over to federal authorities."

Charlcie sneered impatiently, "The authorities won't listen. They think the professor is a nut."

"He's most certainly not a nut!" Brandon snapped. "I should know; I am, or was, as the case may be, his student." He lifted his head proudly and folded his arms more tightly.

"That's why I thought you might want to help rescue

27

him," Matthew patiently explained before Charlcie could say something sarcastic.

"Well naturally I do," Brandon hastily replied. He glanced back at the Tudor mansion where he lived. "It's just that I hate sneaking off from Mommy."

"Mommy!" Charlcie howled before Matthew could stop her.

"Yes, Mommy will be very concerned."

"Then why'd you sneak out with that heavy suitcase?" Mary inquired, reaching forward to tap Brandon's bag.

Brandon blinked, amazed by her accuracy. "Well," he sputtered, "I do feel obligated to help my mentor. Professor Nesbit has been most kind to me. Only he could have taught me as much as I know about quantum physics."

"Bag it, Brandon," Charlcie snarled. "Are you coming or not?"

Brandon sniffed. "As you perhaps have observed, I am packed. I simply wished to ascertain whether federal or state authorities have been notified. . . ."

"They have," Charlcie cut in, moving in the direction of the Nesbit cottage. "But they won't do anything. It's up to us."

"Oh, well, if you put it like that," Brandon said, lifting his suitcase about an inch off the ground and struggling to follow the other three. He looked warily at Fongo. "Does that beast have to accompany us?"

"Unless *you* can protect us from the kidnappers." Charlcie chuckled.

"Me? I assure you that violence is not one of my strong points."

28

"Then shut up about Fongo," Charlcie ordered as they turned onto the road that led out of town.

Within fifteen minutes the four children, Fongo, and six mice were standing in a semicircle inside Professor Nesbit's barn. In front of them was the shiny chrome bumper and oval grill of the red Responder.

"Are you sure you can make that thing run?" Brandon queried.

"I can't make it run at all," Charlcie answered with a gleam in her eyes.

Brandon was a bit slow on the uptake, but then he smiled. "Oh, you mean that it will fly, not run. Ha, ha. The question is, how can you make it fly? The Responder was one of the professor's best kept secrets, even from us."

Charlcie went to the driver's side of the car. She pulled out the red cape, and came forward wrapped in its bright crimson glow. Brandon's eyes opened wide. He whispered, "She's not going to try to use the cape, is she?"

"How else can we fly the Responder?" Charlcie asked with mock sweetness. "There isn't a textbook on Responders, you know."

Brandon clamped his mouth shut as Charlcie tied the cape around her neck. She took a deep breath and said, "Let's load up."

The boys put the suitcases in the Responder's trunk. Mary moved toward Charlcie. Mary had been smiling ever since Charlcie had taken out the cape. Now she clapped her hands and reached unerringly to the red glow. "It's so lovely and warm," she murmured. "It feels like love."

29

Charlcie smiled and nodded, stroking the cape. "I think that's how it controls the Responder."

"But," Brandon began, struggling to lift his suitcase, "can you control the cape?"

Charlcie leveled her gaze on Brandon. "No one controls the cape. I thought you knew that."

"What I meant was," Brandon said, reaching for Mary's suitcase while Matthew loaded Charlcie's, "how will you use it to fly the Responder?"

Charlcie frowned, staring at the long hood of the sleek automobile. "I don't know exactly," she admitted. "The only time the professor took us flying was at night. But the instruments were brightly lit. I think I remember what he switched and turned. The only thing is. . . ."

"That he never flew it with the cape," Matthew concluded, closing the trunk with a bang.

They stared in silence at the Responder. Finally a tiny voice spoke up. It was Padlock.

"Nothing ventured," he said cheerfully as he hoisted his seed pod suitcase, "nothing gained."

"True," Charlcie agreed. "Let's push it out."

The four children and six mice strained to roll the Responder from its stall. When it was moving, Charlcie opened the left door and slid into the driver's seat. She turned the small, black steering wheel to guide the auto into the middle of the barn where it faced the open doors. Outside the doors lay the sunlit crest of the hill which fell sharply toward the road alongside the Nesbit cottage.

On the other side of the road was old Mr. McCutchen's woodlot, a forest of dark pine, fir, and hemlock, most of which were sixty feet tall. The children and mice stared at the thick forest.

Finally, Brandon could stand it no longer. Wiping sweat from his forehead, he asked, "What if it won't start?"

"We'll roll it down the hill to start it," Charlcie decided.

Brandon removed his glasses and began to nervously polish them. "What if it doesn't start? What if we smash into those trees?"

"Brandon-dear," Charlcie grinned, "you'll what-if yourself to death."

"I'll also crash to death if you can't start the Responder," Brandon cried angrily, stamping his foot in the straw and dust. A mouse coughed.

"I know what to do," Charlcie assured him, "At least I think I do. Just start pushing, then jump in while we're rolling."

Brandon considered the situation without moving a muscle. Then he snapped his fingers and said, "We'd better put the top down so we can jump in more easily."

"That's the best thing you've said yet," Charlcie began. She stopped talking when the glow from the red cape flooded more warmly over her.

Matthew grinned and helped Brandon unlatch the white convertible top and fold it into the boot. They snapped the cover over it and stood back. "Ready?" Matthew asked.

"Not yet," Brandon said. "Mary, why don't you and the mice get in so we won't all have to scramble when it starts to roll?"

"Another good idea!" Matthew said, grinning at his sister.

The mice scampered into the car with Mary, who reached out to squeeze Charlcie's hand. Then Matthew and Brandon strained hard against the rear of the Responder.

"Contact!" Brandon called to Charlcie.

"Contact?" Matthew asked.

Brandon shrugged. "That's what old-time ground crews used to say to pilots."

"Contact!" Charlcie called back, flipping switches and letting out the clutch.

Brandon and Matthew sweated and strained. Fongo, who rarely did anything without a reason, ran and jumped over the trunk; the weight of his huge body landing in the back seat started the Responder rolling. Both boys kept pushing until the car rolled out of the barn and over the hill. Then the boys jumped onto the running boards. Charlcie frantically spread the cape out behind her so the wind fanned it across the Responder. In seconds they were bouncing downhill at twenty miles per hour heading straight for the road and the trees beyond.

They saw Mrs. Nesbit run out of her cottage. "Be careful!" she called, waving her lace handkerchief. "And don't forget the Oversight Lifter!"

"Oh my!" Charlcie cried, looking frantically for the Oversight Lifter switch.

The wall of dark trees loomed larger and larger as the Responder rushed headlong toward them.

3

Obstacles and Suspicions

They were going thirty miles per hour. Brandon and Matthew leaped into the back seat of the Responder and prepared for a crash. On rolled the automobile, two hundred feet from the trees as Charlcie frantically searched for the vital switch.

"Ah-ha!" she whooped triumphantly. She turned the switch to No. 101, leaned back, and pressed the accelerator. The cape glowed, and the Responder's red intensified. This combined color became brighter and brighter until a stream of red particles whooshed from the rear of the Responder. Suddenly its nose lifted.

Higher and higher it rose until the tops of the trees disappeared from view. Blue sky surrounded the speeding car as the children pressed back against its pleated leather seats. They could not move for several minutes as the wind rushed by them and the red cape flowing behind Charlcie obscured their vision. When they had flown for several minutes, Brandon and Matthew scooted over and looked down.

"Wow!" Matthew cried. "Look at that view!"

Brandon leaned over the side and held his hands beside his eyes so the wind wouldn't whip off his glasses. "There's the professor's barn and cottage," he yelled, "and there's the town. Look! You can see my house!" He turned toward Mary, who was seated in front and facing straight ahead.

Mary giggled. "It feels like we're going awfully fast," she said.

Charlcie looked at the dashboard where instruments registered numbers. "Our airspeed is three hundred forty-six miles per hour," she announced to her passengers. She turned the wheel and sent the Responder into a hard left turn.

"Whoa!" Brandon screamed, grabbing for the door. His face was white. "Don't do that again. I almost fell out!"

Charlcie laughed. "Not quite like an airplane, is it?"

Matthew and Brandon looked around. The Responder popped through puffy white clouds, and the boys saw miniature farmlands, tiny black-lined highways, toy houses, and a hazy horizon. "No," Matthew said, "this is a lot more fun than an airplane! Nothing blocks the view except that cape."

For a moment the Responder hesitated. Charlcie screamed, "Don't say anything bad about the cape!" The auto righted itself and whooshed on.

One by one the mice came out of hiding. But Padlock had to drag out the last two. "Now, Carpettack and Screenspring, you mustn't be frightened," he chided them. "We're among friends." The two mice nodded and sat on the back seat between Brandon and Matthew with Whiskbroom, Doorstop, Lightswitch, and Padlock. But they were still scared stiff, no matter what Padlock said.

"All right crew," Charlcie called over her shoulder, "it's decision-making time. Where do we go?"

Matthew turned to Brandon. "Have you ever heard of a person or place called Kalabashar?"

Brandon signaled to Matthew to wait. He climbed over the back seat to the trunk, opened it, and rummaged inside. With difficulty he managed to open his suitcase and crawl back to his seat with a large book. "Whew!" he gasped, "I'd feel much safer with a parachute."

"Just look up Kalabashar," Matthew said, peering at the book. Its title was *World Atlas of Places and People, Unabridged.*

"Amsterdam, Brazilia," Brandon muttered, thumbing pages with difficulty because of the wind. "Denver, Franco, Kuwait, oops, passed it." He went back a page, then ran his finger down a column. At last he smiled, pushed his glasses up on his nose, and read, "Kalabashar; an Arab emirate in the Red Sea. Land area; 66 square miles. Resources; petroleum." He showed Matthew the island on a map and for Charlcie's benefit added, "It's between Ethiopia and Yemen."

"What's an em . . . emerite?" Charlcie asked, steering the Responder gently through some particularly nice clouds.

Brandon blinked. "It's pronounced e-mir'ate, and means an Arabian military commander."

"So Kalabashar could be both an island and a person," Charlcie concluded.

"Very good." Brandon smiled with mock professorial majesty. "Perhaps I underestimated your intelli., . . ."

"Bag it, Brandon-dear!" Charlcie warned.

Fongo lifted his head from the floorboard and glared at Brandon.

Brandon snapped his book shut and glanced from Fongo to Matthew and back to Fongo. "Now, listen, I won't be threatened by your sister and that beast," he cried.

"Go back to sleep," Matthew said to Fongo, patting his large white head. Then Matthew grinned. "Relax, Brandon. Just re-lax!"

"I smell something awful," Mary said suddenly. She raised her head into the wind, sniffed, and nodded. "It might just be the exhaust from a jet, but it smells more awful than that."

Charlcie frowned. "How could that be?"

Brandon glanced at his wristwatch. "Even though it's been three hours since the kidnappers left, perhaps the high level winds are calm enough to hold traces of the rocket's exhaust."

"Which direction does the smell go?" Charlcie asked.

Mary sniffed this way and that. Her long, glossy black hair streamed out behind her. "I can't say for sure, but the trail seems to go north."

"North?" Brandon inquired. "But Kalabashar lies due east. Why wouldn't the kidnappers go east?"

"They'd probably take the polar route." Matthew said. "Surely even you know that route would be faster than the trans-Atlantic one."

Brandon blushed instantly and removed his glasses. They flew in silence until Brandon ventured to say, "It seems to me that since we know the kidnappers' probable destination, pursuit is unnecessary. It might profit us instead to spend time investigating another clue. General Throckmorton." Brandon thumbed through his thick book again. "Ah," he said at last, "here he is. General Hunnicutt Throckmorton, Commanding General of the United States Air Force, youngest Air Force officer—"

"Wow," Matthew interrupted, "Professor Nesbit didn't mess around. He must have been dealing only with top brass."

Annoyed at the interruption, Brandon dryly said, "That doesn't really surprise you, does it? The police may think the professor is a nut, but *we* know how important his work is. And if we know, then surely people in high places in Washington must know."

"Maybe even the president knows," Mary suggested with a smile. "Maybe the professor was working on something that's important to the whole country!"

Brandon nodded. "It wouldn't surprise me a bit. However, if he *was* working on a top secret project, we won't get much help from Washington."

"They'll just tell us to go home and be good children," Matthew groused.

"In any case, General Throckmorton needs to be told about the kidnapping," Charlcie decided. "Brandon, can you guide us to Washington?"

"Of course I can," Brandon said confidently, "but I'll have to get a map and compass from my suitcase." He looked at the trunk, then at the blue-green ground thousands of feet below. With a shaky breath, he slowly worked his way to the trunk. After a few moments of digging, he slid back into his place with a sigh. "Whew! Thought the wind had me there for a moment." He glared at Matthew. "You might at least have held on to my feet!"

"Sorry," Matthew mumbled, watching Brandon open his map. Matthew held one side of it so the wind wouldn't whip it out of his hands. Brandon brushed his pale blond hair away from his eyes and positioned his compass. "Steer left until I tell you to stop," he called to Charlcie. She steered left until he yelled, "Stop! Now we're heading due east. Keep going for about a thousand miles."

"Okay," Charlcie agreed, "hang on while I shift gears."

"Shift gears?" Brandon cried. "Why?"

"We're cruising in second gear at 403 miles per hour. I'll watch the altitude so we don't get too high and run out of oxygen. You two pass around our sack lunches and watch for airplanes."

The boys were silent as Charlcie shifted gears. The Responder shot forward. She shifted again. Clouds swept past. The wind began to scream over the windshield. All the mice disappeared under the front seat, and Fongo whined. "It's all right," Matthew reassured the great wolf, "Charlcie knows what she's doing."

"I certainly hope so," Brandon muttered, slipping his glasses into his shirt pocket so they wouldn't get blown away.

The red cape's glow fired up, and the trail of red particles from the rear of the Responder streamed for miles as the sleek auto flashed east. When the bright red machine reached top speed, it seemed to be flying

38

with the wind. In fact, it was flying much faster than the wind.

Dulles International Airport is usually a calm, uneventful place. But when its air traffic controllers found an unidentified blip on their radar screens, they began to get excited. The blip was signaled, then frantically signaled again. When there was no reply, the controllers alerted the Air Force, concluding that the capital was under attack. An entire squadron of jet fighters roared into the sky to intercept the object.

"Dulles tower, Dulles tower," the squadron commander radioed in a few minutes, "this is Colonel Scanlon, F-114-204. Do you copy?"

"We copy. What've you got?" the Dulles supervisor asked.

The radio crackled with static, then Colonel Scanlon replied, "You're not going to believe this."

"What is it? A Russian spy jet? A UFO?"

"Well, not exactly," Colonel Scanlon said, sending his jet in a screaming turn alongside the red object. "It's an automobile."

"A *what*?"

"An automobile. Four children are flying it, and a large white dog is snarling at me from the back seat."

There was a moment of silence. Then the supervisor snapped, "Colonel, have you been drinking?"

"No, sir," the commander returned sharply. "I'm seeing something I can't believe myself. I'll force them to land."

No force was necessary. The 1924 Responder swooped low over Pennsylvania Avenue, circled the Washington Monument, crossed the Potomac River, and positioned itself over the main runway of Dulles International. In minutes, flanked by howling F-114's, the bright red car touched down. Smoke puffed from its tires as it rolled to a stop.

Emergency vehicles and airport security police raced onto the runway with sirens wailing. Soon they surrounded the Responder and its startled passengers. The auto slowly moved to the arches of the terminal building.

"All right," boomed a voice from a police car, "whoever and whatever you are, get out with your hands up!"

As the police came to get Charlcie, Matthew, and their friends, Fongo growled menacingly. Charlcie stepped out, drew the red cape tightly around her shoulders, and stared at the uniformed men. The men tensed with they saw Fongo's bared fangs. "Don't you hurt him!" Charlcie commanded when some police aimed their guns at the wolf.

Eventually the children were taken by police caravan into the city. The Responder was examined by airport security people. When they decided it was harmless, they pushed it into a small hangar and locked it up until scientists from the Defense department could have a look at it. No one saw the mice.

"What do you mean, 'a flying car'?" the police captain demanded.

"Just what I said," the chief of airport security police repeated impatiently. "Ask the Air Force, they'll confirm it."

"They'd better," the police captain huffed. He dialed a number on the telephone as he glared suspiciously at the four children and their wolf. "Hello, Pentagon?

This is Captain Johnson of the District Police Department. I need to speak with General Throckmorton. I'm sure he *is* busy, but we've got a strange situation down here. I can assure you the general will want to know about it!"

Within an hour General Hunnicutt Throckmorton and six staff officers were standing in front of the cell where the children and Fongo had been confined.

"They certainly don't look dangerous," the general said with a smile.

"They caused a ruckus by landing at Dulles," the colonel muttered. His expression was a mixture of anger and perplexity. "The entire 204th Tactical Squadron was scrambled."

"Now, now," General Throckmorton said gently, looking at the very dejected children. Charlcie got up from the bunk bed in the cell and went to the bars.

"Could we please speak to you alone?" she asked the general.

He smiled again. "Yes, I believe so." He signaled his officers to leave the room. "Don't worry," the general said. "Children are children, even if they have flown into Dulles International by car."

When the staff officers and policemen left, Charlcie whispered, "You know it's not just a red car, don't you?"

General Throckmorton dragged a chair over to the cell door. He pushed his gold-braided hat back on his head and loosened his tie. "It's a 1924 Responder with a top speed of 700 miles per hour, but range indefinite." He grinned. "Now tell me how you came to be flying it in broad daylight."

"Professor Nesbit's been kidnapped," Charlcie explained quickly.

"The police won't do anything about it!" Matthew added, wrapping his hands around two bars.

"They think he's a nut," Charlcie put in before the general could say anything.

"But we and you know he's not!" Matthew concluded, nodding sharply.

General Throckmorton stopped smiling. "When was he kidnapped?"

Charlcie and Matthew told him the story. Mary and Brandon moved close to the bars. Charlcie finished, "We think Dirk and Tirk flew Professor Nesbit to Kalabashar."

The general sat back, smoothing his black mustache. "What makes you think that?"

"Lightswitch heard them," Matthew said.

"Who?" General Throckmorton asked.

"Someone who was in the barn at the time of the kidnapping," Matthew whispered, "heard Dirk and Tirk say Kalabashar would be glad they finally had the professor."

"Perhaps your friend heard wrong," the general muttered.

"Shouldn't you at least investigate Kalabashar?" Charlcie asked, squinting at the general.

Throckmorton laughed suddenly and leaned back. "Certainly," he said. "It's a matter for the CIA to handle. I'll get in touch with them at once." He stood up.

The children banged their fists on the bars. "Wait!" Charlcie protested. "You're not going to leave us here, are you?"

"I'm afraid I'll have to," the general said slowly, frowning at them. "There are charges against you."

"What charges?" Charlcie demanded, becoming angry and frustrated.

"Flying an improperly identified aircraft, flying without radio in controlled airspace, landing without permission, and," the general said as he moved away, "running away from home."

"But we didn't run away!" Matthew yelled toward the general's back. "We were just trying to find the professor!"

"He'll be found," the general said casually. He stroked his mustache as he went out the cell-block door. After he had talked to the police and officers, he left. The police glared at the children. Then the heavy steel door clanged shut.

Charlcie looked at Brandon and Matthew. Mary felt her way to the bunk bed and began to cry. Charlcie and Matthew went to comfort her. "I guess our adventure is over," Mary said sadly.

They waited, helpless and discouraged. Silence was broken only by Mary's weeping. Charlcie wrapped Mary in the red cape and the young girl stopped crying. Now there was only silence in the cell block.

Padlock's Justice

"It's just not fair!" cried Matthew for the tenth time in three hours. Then he lost his temper completely and kicked the bars. Now his foot hurt so bad he almost started to cry.

Charlcie looked calmly at her brother, then said, "The question is, how are we going to get out of here?"

Matthew tried to rattle the bars but they wouldn't move. He became furious. "Let us out of here!" he screamed. "We didn't know we were breaking the law, and we didn't hurt anybody!"

"Oh, do be quiet," Brandon sighed. "I'm trying to think of a way. Say!" He snapped his fingers. "We ought to call the American Civil Liberties Union. They could get us sprung on a writ of habeas corpus ad subjiciendum." He looked smugly at Charlcie.

Charlcie stared at Brandon, then looked at her brother. "It won't do any good for anyone to get mad. And Brandon's way will take too long. By the time lawyers get us out of here, Kalabashar will have brainwashed the professor."

Matthew persisted. "But the police don't have any right to hold us! And we should at least have been allowed to make a phone call."

"Right or not," Charlcie said evenly, "they are holding us. No matter who we call, we couldn't get out of here fast enough. What we need to do is follow Dirk and Tirk before their trail is cold."

Brandon sat down with a sigh. "I don't think we have to worry about them or the professor anymore. The Central Intelligence Agency will find them."

"Oh?" Charlcie asked, lifting her eyebrows. "You trust General Throckmorton, do you?"

"Certainly!" Brandon snapped.

"Well I don't," Charlcie asserted. "Something's fishy. He knows a lot more than he'll admit, and he left us here so we wouldn't interfere with Kalabashar."

"Oh, baloney," Brandon muttered, putting his elbows on his knees and propping his face on his hands. "What makes you think that?"

"I don't know exactly," Charlcie said in a low voice. "I guess I just don't like the way he stroked his mustache when he said, 'He'll be found.' "

"Maybe the professor and General Throckmorton are working with Kalabashar on some top secret project and we're not supposed to get in the way," Brandon speculated. "I just can't see an Air Force general getting this involved."

"I wish we had the Truthfall machine," Matthew griped. "That would show who was lying and who wasn't."

Charlcie tisked. "Sometimes I wish I'd come alone."

"Yeah?" Matthew sneered. "Well, I haven't heard

you come up with any great ideas about getting us free. It's not fair, I tell you!'' he screamed toward the steel door of their cell block.

Charlcie slumped on the bunk. After a while she realized that Mary, who was still wrapped in the red cape, hadn't said a word during the argument. "Mary?" Charlcie asked gently. "What do you think we should do?"

Mary turned her dark, unseeing eyes toward Charlcie. "You'd laugh at me if I told you what I do when things seem impossible."

"*Seem* impossible?" Matthew laughed. "They *are* impossible!"

"See?" Mary whispered, slumping under the cape.

"Don't pay any attention to him," Charlcie said. "He's just mad because he can't get his way with a tantrum."

Mary sighed. Then she began to smile. As she smiled the red cape began to glow. "What I always do when things get rough is pray."

Brandon's head jerked up. "Prayer is a nonrational substitute for clear thinking."

Matthew frowned. "If you think it'll get us out of jail, I'll pray with you."

Mary shook her head. "It doesn't work like that. That's trying to make a deal with God."

Matthew paced back to the bars.

"I'll pray with you," Charlcie said firmly. She took Mary's right hand and held it as Mary prayed.

The next hour passed slowly. Matthew and Brandon talked about escape, but each of their ideas had flaws, and all the while they worried about what was happen-

47

ing to the professor. Then suddenly the steel door of the cell swung open. Bright light flooded the room.

Matthew and Brandon stared at the light and wondered if a miracle was happening.

"Look here," a man's voice yelled. "My camera crew and I represent NBC! Do you have any idea how the nation will react when our evening news opens with the story of how district police and Air Force officials are holding four children in jail?"

A police officer backed into the cell block, helplessly trying to hold back a man who was carrying television spotlights. More men followed, one with a camera on his shoulder, one with a tape recorder, and another with curly brown hair and a microphone in his hand. The man holding the microphone thrust it toward the police officer. "Go on, Mr. Armbruster, tell the nation how four children were held for four hours without legal counsel and without making a telephone call." But Mr. Armbruster escaped past the television crew and out of the cell.

The tall, brown haired man laughed as he led his crew to the children. "Don't worry, kids. We'll get you out of here. Just tell us your story!"

Charlcie acted as spokesperson for the group, but she refused to give any details about the kidnapping, Responder, or suspicions regarding General Throckmorton. By the time the interview was over, six official-looking men entered the cell block. Two of them presented papers which ordered the release of the children. Apologies were made while the cameraman moved in to get close-ups of the embarrassed faces of Washington officials. Then the children left the jail.

Outside the building the curly-haired news reporter said, "My name's Robert Downing." Then he whispered, "Now you can tell me the *real* story."

Charlcie exchanged looks with Matthew and Brandon as she held Mary's hand. "There really isn't any more to tell."

"Nonsense!" Robert Downing motioned away his sound technician and camerman so he could talk privately. "Listen. Something very unusual is going on. I've talked with six people who saw you land that red car at Dulles International. One of the jailers told me you were locked up so you wouldn't interfere in a kidnap case involving one of America's leading scientists. So please cooperate. NBC will offer you $500,000 for exclusive rights to your story."

Charlcie blinked. She looked at Brandon and Matthew. Both were wide-eyed with wonder, but neither said a word. "I'll tell you what, Mr. Downing," Charlcie whispered. "If you help us get our automobile back so we can leave Washington, you'll get exclusive rights to our story as soon as we succeed with our mission."

"Which is?" Robert asked, squatting on a step.

"We can't tell you now," Charlcie hedged.

"How can I help you if I don't know what's going on?" Mr. Downing asked suspiciously. "You might be spies."

"You'll just have to trust us," Charlcie said firmly.

Mr. Downing looked at the children, one by one. Finally he looked at Fongo. Then he said, "You kids I trust. *Him,*" he pointed at the wolf, "I don't."

Charlcie smiled and stuck out her hand. "Deal?" she asked.

"Deal," Mr. Downing repeated, shaking her hand emphatically. He motioned for his crew to pack up their equipment and get the staff car.

While the children waited for the car, Brandon's curiosity got the best of him. "How'd you find us?"

Robert combed his thick brown curls with his fingers. "It was the strangest thing. I was sitting in the office about three hours ago when I felt the urge to call a friend who works at Dulles. I hardly said hello when he began yelling about four kids who had landed in a red automobile. He said he called two other reporters but they just laughed at him. So I called around until I found out where you were taken. When I told the facts to my boss, he authorized the fee for an exclusive story." Robert looked at Charlcie. "He said he might even do a movie on this if you manage to do whatever it is you're trying to do."

"How did you get the charges against us dropped?" Brandon asked.

"Charges?" Robert repeated. "There weren't any. Who'd charge four juveniles with landing an automobile at Dulles? Any judge in the country would laugh the case out of court."

Brandon looked at Matthew, then at Charlcie. Slowly they turned to Mary. She was smiling, peaceful and confident, as if she knew all along this would happen.

Then Brandon coughed, frowned, and tugged on Robert's sleeve. "Wouldn't you say it was an incredible coincidence that you stumbled onto our story?"

"Coincidence? I wouldn't say that at all."

"Just a reporter's instinct for news?" Brandon persisted.

50

"Well maybe," Robert hedged. "But I really couldn't say what made me pick up the phone to call my friend, or what made me take such an outlandish story to my superior and bring a crew down here. Reporter's instincts? Maybe. Maybe not."

The car arrived and the four children plus Fongo piled into the back seat while the men crowded in up front. After thirty minutes of fighting heavy traffic, they arrived at Dulles International.

Robert Downing was so tall, impressive, and fast-talking that the airport authorities were no match for him. He talked his way right into the chief of airport operations office with camera, recorder, and lights. But there he was stopped.

"No, Mr. Downing. I don't care if you represent all three networks," the chief said firmly. "We can't release that automobile to you or anyone else. The Air Force has impounded it until a thorough investigation has been completed." The man folded his arms and closed his eyes against the glare of hot white camera lights.

Mr. Downing wouldn't take no for an answer. He argued and argued. While he argued, Charlcie led the children and Fongo out of the office. They slipped through a crowd that had gathered and ran down a deserted hallway. At the end of the hall was a door marked "Authorized Flight Personnel Only/Fire Exit."

"We're not authorized," she whispered, "but we are flight personnel." She grinned and pushed open the door.

Immediately an alarm went off. That brought security police on the run, but they found nothing more than an open door. After a thorough search they went back inside, locking the door behind them.

From behind the canvas curtain of a baggage car a head with blue eyes, pert nose, and long auburn hair cautiously emerged. Slowly Charlcie Arrow stepped out, summoning her friends. Along the side of the building they ran, straight toward the hangars where private aircraft were kept. Then suddenly Charlcie stopped. The others piled into each other.

"Air Force police!" she hissed, peeking around a corner. "They're guarding that hangar." She pointed to a small building. The children sat down. Fongo panted in the humid heat.

"Now what do we do?" Matthew asked. He scuffed the pavement with one shoe. "It's just not fair."

Charlcie cut him off. "I'm tired of hearing about how unfair everything is. Now shut up and let me catch my breath."

"What for?" Brandon asked. He watched several vehicles loaded with passengers roll out to waiting airplanes. No one saw the children hiding near the hangar.

Charlcie began to whistle a merry, springtime tune.

"The mice?" Matthew asked. "Of course!" He turned to help Brandon keep watch.

Charlcie's tune drifted sweetly through the air, but she stopped whistling when Matthew grabbed her arm. Several men in jumpsuits rumbled past on tractors pulling lines of baggage cars. Fortunately the men were so intent on their business that they didn't see the children. But one train almost ran over a tiny gray and brown mouse that skittered across the pavement.

"Whew!" Padlock whistled. "That was close. Hi-ya!"

"Hello Padlock," Charlcie grinned, using the tip of her finger to stroke the mouse's back. He sat up and vigorously rubbed his whiskers. "Is the Responder okay?" she asked.

"Sure," Padlock replied. "We've been guarding it. Everybody is afraid to touch it."

"Is that building locked?" Matthew asked.

"Tighter than the professor's secret footlocker," Padlock replied.

"Let's sic Fongo on them," Brandon suggested.

Matthew patted the wolf's head. "He's been trained to guard, not attack," he explained.

"Do you have any better suggestions?" Brandon asked snippishly.

Matthew frowned, peering at the hangar. "No, but it makes me mad that they've locked up the Responder. They don't have any right to."

"You want the Responder out?" Padlock asked, blinking his bright black eyes.

"Sure, but what can you do?" Matthew looked worried as another train of baggage handlers rattled past.

"Simple," Padlock snickered, sprinting off in a zig-zag toward the hangar.

Minutes later four mice appeared under the corrugated metal door of the building. Cautiously they approached four guards who were talking among themselves. Two were sitting smoking cigarettes, and one was jingling a ring of keys which hung from his belt on a leather strap. Suddenly, three guards leaped up. Two burned themselves with cigarettes as they hopped

53

up and down, and the one with the keys fell to the ground. The children giggled as the guard on the ground tried to pull off his pants to remove a mouse that was racing up and down his leg.

In a jiffy two other mice raced over to the guard. As he ripped off his pants and grabbed his shorts for one mouse, two others neatly bit his ring of keys off its leather strap.

The children broke from cover and raced to the guards. In seconds Charlcie had the keys. She read the name on the hangar door lock, then found a matching key on the ring.

Meanwhile tragedy struck. One of the guards shook Carpettack from his pants and stomped on him. Then he drew his gun. He pointed it at Charlcie and yelled, "Don't touch that lock!"

Fongo leaped up and seized the man's gun arm in his long jaws. Then he pushed him to the ground. The man stared at the snarling wolf without moving a muscle. The other guards froze too.

Charlcie snapped open the lock. Matthew and Brandon each took a side of the corrugated metal door and slid it open. Quickly the children raced to the Responder and helped the mice inside. As Charlcie flipped the start switch, Mary took the red cape off her shoulders and tied it around Charlcie's neck. The cape and Responder began to glow as the engine whined. When Charlcie moved the Oversight Lifter switch the glow grew brighter and brighter, but now the boys wondered if they would have to push the auto to get it moving. Suddenly however, the bright red machine burst from the hangar, whooshing past the startled guards. At the last moment, Fongo leaped into the back seat.

The Air Force guards aimed guns at the speeding auto, but its exhaust of red glowing particles blinded them. They staggered around and bumped into each other as the Responder taxied to a runway.

A gigantic Boeing 747 screeched to a halt as the red auto darted under its nose and took off. The pilot stared in disbelief as this *car* soared into bright blue sky. Once again the children were flying with the wind.

"I hope the guards don't get into too much trouble," Mary said.

"I hope they do," Matthew yelled. "It would serve 'em right!"

Padlock popped up next to Fongo and looked sadly at Matthew. "Don't forget Carpettack."

The children were suddenly silent, lost in thought. Matthew wished they could have gotten the Responder back without anyone getting hurt. Brandon fretted about Robert Downing and Mary's prayer. Had Downing's investigation been coincidence, reporter's instinct, or what? Charlcie worried about General Throckmorton, the CIA, and Kalabashar. Just who was doing what to whom? Only Mary was smiling. The air smelled delicious, the wind cooled her cheeks, and she alone was certain that God had answered her prayer.

5

Pintor's Relief

Northward they flew, swifter than eagles. On their left, Saturday's sunset splashed orange and red over the dark lumps of Appalachian Mountains. On their right shone the lights of east coast cities and the steely-blue vastness of the Atlantic Ocean.

"Fighters!" Brandon screamed, looking back. He disregarded the wind which almost tore his glasses off.

Charlcie glanced back, her red cape streaming like a flame. The Responder's exhaust trailed a crimson streak which six Air Force jets with flashing green and red lights were following. They roared past at supersonic speed, their pilots straining eyes in disbelief as they watched this car soar north at half their speed. The jets broke formation and turned abruptly into the blue-black sky.

"Here they come again!" Brandon warned.

"I hear them," Charlcie shouted, looking at the dashboard. She remembered once the professor had called attention to something interesting. He had simply stopped the car by pushing *something*.

"They're here!" Brandon yelled.

Charlcie pushed the Oversight Lifter switch to No. 302, and the Responder stopped in midair.

Six Air Force F-114's shot past with an ear-splitting roar. Charlcie switched the Oversight Lifter to No. 182, hit the accelerator, and nosed the Responder down. Before the jets could circle back the red automobile was diving toward the ground at top speed.

"Stop!" Brandon cried as he pounded against the front seat. The lights of New York City rushed toward them. It seemed inevitable they would crash into brightly lit towers of concrete, glass, and steel.

Charlcie pulled back hard on the steering wheel and sent the Responder roaring over the Avenue of the Americas. People on sidewalks, cars, and taxis raced for cover, but before they knew where the red glow came from, the 1924 Responder had shot past Manhattan Island. Air Force jets searched the night sky in vain. Charlcie eased off the accelerator, and the Responder's red exhaust faded. Straight ahead she saw a broad boulevard leading from Manhattan Island to the Hudson River. She guided the auto to a place where there was little traffic and set its wheels down gently. Once it was on the ground, the Responder seemed nothing more than an expensive antique car. Its Chinese red paint, sweeping fenders, chrome bumpers, and oval grill were elegant but at home in the big city.

"What are we doing here?" Matthew finally asked. "What does it look like?" Charlcie demanded, frustrated with driving through the maze of streets choked with traffic. She studiously avoided the eyes of pedestrians, cab drivers, and policemen. "We're sort of hiding."

"Well, get us out of here."

It was too late. A police siren wailed behind them.

"Take off!" Matthew yelled.

"The fighters are waiting for us," Charlcie explained, urging the Responder around corner after corner. The speeding car shot under an elevated train track and suddenly faced a wall of traffic. Charlcie looked back. Now there were four police cars in pursuit with blue lights flashing. She hit the Oversight Lifter switch and the Responder soared over the traffic jam. Drivers hung out of car windows, gawking as the sleek red auto sailed ten feet above them. One lady stood up through her sunroof and lost her wig to the wind whooshing from the red auto. Soon Charlcie brought the car down onto a narrow street, made a hard right onto Fifth Avenue, and slammed on the brakes. "I don't know where else to go!" she cried.

Brandon rummaged for another book in his suitcase. "City maps," he nodded to Matthew. By the light of street lamps he examined the tangled maze of New York City. "Ah ha!" he shouted. "Keep going down Fifth Avenue. Central Park's up ahead. Maybe we can hide there until the fuss is over."

Charlcie doubted the fuss would end soon; nevertheless, she pushed the accelerator to guide the Responder through heavy evening traffic. When she glanced at apartment houses on her right, she almost hit a Rolls Royce pulling into the driveway of the Pierre Hotel. Suddenly she saw the entrance to the zoo, and swerving wildly across six lanes of traffic, brought the car finally onto a narrow service drive into the park.

Near a rocky hill covered with trees Charlcie parked and turned off the Responder. Its red glow faded slowly. Only a few people in the park paused to look at it, then strolled on, probably thinking the car was part of a movie set. As the darkness of night settled around them, the children found themselves alone. Little did they know that the park was deserted because it was a dangerous place to be at night.

"Let's get something to eat," Mary proposed. "I smell hamburgers frying east of here."

"I'll go," Matthew volunteered.

"Take Fongo with you," Charlcie suggested. "I'm sure he needs a walk."

Matthew whistled to the white wolf. Fongo obeyed eagerly, trotting alongside Matthew.

Before Matthew and Fongo left the park they met a fierce-looking man walking a pair of Doberman pinschers. Fongo approached the pinschers for a sniff, but the dogs took one look at him and raced away.

Matthew located the hamburger stand but was outraged at having to pay $10, his entire week's allowance, for five hamburgers and a bag of peanuts. He was still steaming as he and Fongo walked back into Central Park.

"Help!" a man shouted. "Please, somebody help me!" The man sounded like he was terrified, and Matthew unhesitatingly set off after him. His bag of food flopped up and down as Matthew approached a baseball diamond, and saw a gang of teenagers threatening a well-dressed black man. The man's hands were raised to ward off blows from baseball bats.

"Get 'em, Fongo," Matthew whispered.

Fongo needed no more than one command. His first master, Matthew's father, had found him in northern Alaska where the wolf had saved him from an angry grizzly bear. Now Fongo responded just as he had when he faced the grizzly, silently hurling himself at the gang. Before they could scream their bats were smashed from their hands. Soon they were running off in all directions.

The black man slowly sat up. "Thanks," he said with a groan. Matthew helped the man to his feet and brushed off his suit. The man laughed nervously. "Young man, I'd be dead if it weren't for your animal's assistance. How can I repay you?"

Matthew considered this offer while Fongo nosed around. He was still thinking as he led the man to the Responder. He asked, "Would you like a hamburger?"

"No, thank you," the man answered, adjusting his tie and vest. "But if you like, I'll buy you a much better supper. I know about an excellent restaurant."

"Who are you?" Charlcie asked, getting out of the Responder.

The man stared at the automobile. He circled around it, peering at its shiny sides and curved fenders. Then he examined the auto's surroundings, New York's Central Park. "What's this doing here?" he stammered.

"Sorry, I asked first," Charlcie said pleasantly.

"Oh, yes," the man said, swallowing. He shook his head and sat down on the running board. "First let me catch my breath. I've just had a rather trying experience."

The children passed around hamburgers, and Matthew spread peanuts on the back seat for the mice, who, led by Padlock, each claimed a peanut.

The man stared at the mice and rubbed his forehead as though he had a splitting headache. "I must be dreaming," he muttered. He shook his head. "I didn't drink that much with dinner, did I?"

Matthew and Charlcie laughed. "Sir, you're really all right," said Charlcie. "We're just tourists. You know how strange tourists can be."

"To be sure," the man said, seemingly relieved. "Well now, as to your question, my name is Pintor Yarim. I am a delegate to the United Nations from Ethiopia."

"Ethiopia!" Brandon exlaimed, sitting next to the man on the running board. He offered the delegate a bite of his hamburger but Pintor Yarim politely declined. Brandon continued, "Isn't Ethiopia close to the island of Kalabashar?"

"Yes, it is," Pintor replied with a frown. "Why do you ask?"

"Kalabashar is very important to us."

Pintor's frown deepened. "Kalabashar is an awful place. It's causing lots of problems for my nation and Arab nations east of the Red Sea. In fact, many nations in the world are worried about what's going on in Kalabashar."

All the children gathered around the diplomat. Charlcie swallowed the last of her hamburger and asked, "Why are you worried about Kalabashar?"

"The place is ruled by a madman with the same name as the island," Pintor said. He seemed to lose his train of thought then, as the events of the evening brought his eyes back to the red automobile. He shook his head. "I should have listened to the doorman," he muttered, "and not left the hotel!"

"Oh, no, sir," said Mary, leaning over the side of the car. "You must realize you were brought to us for a very special reason. Never mind about how strange everything seems and just play along with us."

Pintor Yarim smiled. "Okay, I'll try." He rubbed a bruise on his shoulder. "I won't feel much like playing when I wake up in the morning."

"No," Matthew said, "I don't imagine you will. But will you please tell us more now about Kalabashar?"

"What I know about Kalabashar, the man, is based on sketchy intelligence reports. He claims to be a Muslim caliph or religious ruler. He says all the Arabs should obey his orders to withhold petroleum from Western nations. His goal is to bring Europe and North America to their knees. His spokesman rants daily on Kalabashar's radio station that the Arabs should begin a holy war to wipe out Israel, then attack the rest of the nations of the Western world." He looked closely at the children. "Do you see how dangerous the man is?"

"Absolutely," Charlcie exclaimed.

"Definitely," Brandon agreed, "but how does he plan to achieve his goal?"

"No one is quite sure," Pintor said. "That's why my nation and others are concerned. Ordinarily we would ignore such a person. He's a madman. But unfortunately, he is beginning to demonstrate some strange powers."

"Like what?" Matthew asked.

Pintor stared off into space, then his eyes became

hard. "We hear rumors of an enormous fortress being built under the island by slave labor."

"Slave labor?" Charlcie cried, astonished. "In this day and age?"

"Yes. These slaves are believed to have been acquired from staged rebellions in Africa and Arab nations. During these skirmishes many people have disappeared. Other missing people have been reported to UN delegates too; scientists and technicians who have simply vanished from their countries. Now we have learned that some were taken away by rocketship."

"Does Kalabashar have the technology to build a rocketship?" Brandon inquired.

"In the beginning he didn't. His island was nothing more than sand dunes, coastline, and rocky mountains barren of vegetation. Its original inhabitants made a living by servicing ships on the Red Sea, and by fishing. Then Kalabashar came to the island and discovered huge oil deposits. With that discovery all visible activity on the island stopped. It is believed all Kalabashar's natives have gone underground. And we strongly suspect Kalabashar has captured scientists and technicians from all over the world to build his rocketships and missiles."

"Missiles?" Charlcie said weakly.

"Yes," Pintor sighed. "The whole matter has been seriously discussed in the UN's General Assembly. It was there that Iran, Saudia Arabia, and other oil-producing countries admitted that Kalabashar's threats are already being put into action. In Teheran an oil refinery was blown up by a missile. In Syria an oil pipeline was demolished."

"But why haven't we heard about any of this in the newspapers?" Brandon demanded, jerking his glasses up on his nose.

Pintor patted the crimson side of the Responder. "Why haven't I heard about *this*?"

"The two subjects are not comparable," Brandon replied.

"No," Pintor admitted, "but all nations including the United States and its allies have made a considerable effort to keep this matter quiet. Can you imagine what would happen if the world knew that its entire way of life was threatened by a madman? If Kalabashar's plan succeeds, the world's supply of oil will be drastically limited. Panic, bloodshed, and war may erupt, despite every effort of the UN and other government agencies to stop Kalabashar."

"Oh, no" Mary sighed, slumping against the front seat.

Pintor looked grim. "Not since Hitler has such a threat existed against world security."

"Why are you explaining all this to us?" Brandon wondered.

Pintor put his arm around Matthew. "I owe my life to this young man. What else could I do but tell you what you wanted to know? I also have a strange feeling that I *should* tell you, though I can't imagine why."

Charlcie felt chilled. A tremendous responsibility seemed to be settling onto her shoulders. She wiped sweaty hands on her skirt and pulled the cape close against the nighttime chill. "I have the feeling," she said quietly to the others, "that we may be expected to do the impossible."

Brandon stared at her, feeling his stomach twist. "You can't mean what I think you do. We can't!" he protested, looking desperately at Pintor. "You said the CIA and other secret agencies are trying to stop Kalabashar. Why aren't they?"

"Young man," the delegate said sternly, "would you willingly intrude in an explosive situation dominated by a madman? Kalabashar has kidnapped enough scientists and technicians to produce every kind of weapon there is, including a neutron bomb. Because he's so rich from selling oil from the island, he can afford to build anything his insane mind wants."

"Couldn't someone just blow up the island" Brandon asked nervously, blinking in the blue glow of park lights.

"If you were president of the United States, would you want to be responsible for starting a nuclear chain of explosions which would pollute the atmosphere, destroy vast areas of land, and kill possibly millions of people?"

Brandon shuddered.

"What about commando teams?" Matthew asked. "Surely Israel and the Arab states could provide those."

"They've tried and failed," Pintor stated sadly. "A dozen teams have landed on Kalabashar. None has been heard from since."

"What happened?" Matthew asked in a hushed voice.

Pintor lifted his eyebrows. "I said they were never heard from again. That is why the UN has been meeting nonstop for days, and part of the reason I went to the park tonight for a walk. I had to get away from all that talk about disaster. Unfortunately," he said, "I only found more trouble."

"Not necessarily," Mary said softly.

"What do you mean?" Pintor asked, turning toward her.

Mary faced the delegate. "Help may be closer than you imagine. You were rescued once tonight. You and others concerned about Kalabashar may be helped again."

"How?" Pintor Yarim asked incredulously, pulling white cuffs neatly from his gray coat sleeves.

"With help from agents that you, world leaders, and Kalabashar would never expect," Mary smiled, resting her left hand gently on the man's shoulder.

He started to ask something, then stopped, calmed by her touch. Slowly he began to smile. "I don't know why, but I believe you," he said. "I'm also very relieved. It's the first time in weeks I've felt this way." He reached out to touch each of them on the head. He even patted Fongo.

6

What to Believe?

Matthew and Fongo walked Pintor Yarim to the edge of Central Park. Then Matthew and the wolf raced back to the Responder. "What'd you think of his story?" the boy asked, trying to catch his breath.

Charlcie nestled into the red cape and smiled. "I feel relieved."

"Because we know about a disaster that could wipe out the whole world?" Matthew sputtered.

"No," Charlcie laughed, "because we know more about what's going on. I feel like Mary does; somehow we're supposed to be doing this, even if people like General Throckmorton don't want us to."

"It sounds hopelessly dangerous to me," Brandon said gloomily.

"Matthew said things were hopeless when we were in jail," Mary reminded him, "but here we are." She sat next to Charlcie and wrapped part of the red cape around herself. The cape's glow lit up the girls' faces.

Brandon looked at their smiles and scraped dirt with his foot. "I for one would feel better if we had a rational plan of action."

"Okay, Brandon," Charlcie retorted. "Since you're so awfully smart, you come up with a plan." In the darkness she grinned.

Brandon went to the back seat of the Responder and dug out his flashlight, maps, compass, and books. For a long time he studied and dabbled with figures. Finally he announced, "What we should do is reconnoiter, or scout the area." He became more excited. "We've got to learn how to approach the island. We need to know what weapons Kalabashar used against the commando teams that landed on the island. We need to know his strengths and weaknesses. In short, we need to assess the problem before we can propose alternative solutions."

"All right," Charlcie agreed, "where do we start?"

"I suggest that first we fly over the island to have a look at it. Then we should land at nearby cities to learn what we can from people living there. They would probably know more about our enemy than would secret intelligence agencies." He paused, looking up at the brightly-lit skyscrapers beyond the edge of the park. "Wow," he murmured. "Just think. We may accomplish what the CIA, Interpol, and even Israeli and Arab commandos can't!"

"Let's just concentrate on rescuing the professor," Charlcie said dryly.

"Oh, I know," Brandon returned hastily. "But doesn't the idea of saving the whole world from disaster excite you? Wow! Just think how grateful everybody would be! We'd be heroes!"

"We haven't done it yet," Matthew reminded him, "so don't get too carried away."

"Come on, Matthew," Brandon argued, "you're the

one who's so hot about justice. Aren't you looking forward to stopping a madman who wants to cut off the Western world's petroleum supply and maybe even blow up all of us?" His hands tightened on his books. You talk about something that's not fair!"

"Yeah, well," Matthew mumbled with an uneasy glance at his sister.

"Come on, you guys," Charlcie said. "Let's get going!"

"Whoa," Matthew objected, frowning. "What about food and water?"

"Would I leave home without proper provision for an expedition of indefinite length?" Brandon asked as he settled into the back seat with his books and maps. "You didn't think the weight of my suitcase was merely books, did you?"

"Brandon," Matthew grinned, "it's an effort, but I think I like you."

"Thanks," Brandon answered uncertainly, grabbing the side of the Responder as Charlcie spread the cape behind her and prepared for take-off. In seconds they were airborne.

The brightly-lit towers of Manhattan Island soon dimmed beneath them as the Responder climbed toward the stars. Charlcie glanced down and said, "You know, none of those lights would be burning if it weren't for the electricity we get from oil." Brandon and Matthew also looked down. Seeing the lights of New York and the entire eastern seaboard gave them a tremendous sense of purpose. But their sense of excitement began to fade as they entered the bone-chilling clouds above the steel-gray Atlantic Ocean.

Brandon set their course, and, using his flashlight,

concentrated on his compass to steer them eastward. The red cape glowed behind Charlcie and the auto soon reached maximum speed. Behind it stretched a long tail of particles which glowed like red, phosphorescent dust. The red dust trailed a quarter mile behind, but the children never saw if it touched down to the cold ocean below. They were flying too high and too fast to see anything except stars pushing through dark clouds.

When dawn came, everyone but Charlcie was asleep. Charlcie watched the eerie light, fascinated by the flood of gray light over a towering mass of clouds. Gray lightened to pearl-white, then to a pale yellow haze. Through this yellow haze now came the red light of the sun. Charlcie smiled. The sun was a friendly, warm face after a lonely night.

Soon the others awakened. Brandon passed out food. Even Fongo and the mice had breakfast while Brandon studied his maps. When he had computed their rate of speed, distance, and direction, he announced, "We must be over Africa."

The others were impressed. None of them had ever been outside of the United States. But Charlcie was worried. "Where exactly do you think we are?"

Brandon leaned out to look down. He saw a tan, vast area broken occasionally by blue-green. Far to his left was an endless stretch of blue water. He sat back and brushed his wind-blown hair from his face. "I'm afraid I don't know exactly. But that water to the north is probably the Mediterranean Sea."

"Great," Charlcie muttered. Quickly, she made her own decision. She pushed against the steering wheel. Down went the automobile toward the earth below.

Everyone's ears popped with the sudden loss of altitude. Finally Charlcie pulled back on the steering wheel. As the Responder swooped out of its dive, Matthew and Brandon relaxed enough to look around.

"I see a broad strip of green on each side of a river," Matthew announced happily.

"That's where the river empties into the Mediterranean," Brandon said, pointing. "We must be over Egypt."

"I see a large city," Charlcie added, motioning with her head. "It's near the river's delta."

"That city is probably Cairo," Brandon said. "Let's get a little closer."

Charlcie forced the Responder into another dive which almost took Brandon's breath away. When he was finally able to speak again, he almost yelled in Charlcie's ear, "Look! The pyramids of Giza! That *must* be Cairo."

"Okay, now what?" Charlcie asked.

"Steer to the right and look for a large body of water. That'll be the Red Sea. The island of Kalabashar should be about 800 miles to the south."

Charlcie followed Brandon's directions and before long they spotted the long expanse of the Red Sea. Charlcie boosted the Responder's speed to its maximum, and faster than the wind they sped over specks on the water below. They concluded that the specks were oil tankers. The rising sun sparkled on huge areas of blue around the ships.

"It doesn't look red to me," Matthew observed. "But it does look heavily traveled. Charlcie, can you see all the oil tankers down there?"

Charlcie glanced down. She nodded. "I'll bet the

low-riding ones going north are loaded with oil, and the ones with red paint showing under black hulls are empty ones going south. Where are they going, Kalabashar?"

"Most likely they're going past it toward the Persian Gulf," said Brandon.

Matthew leaned out to look at the sea again. "Say," he offered, frowning, "it looks like the ships are stopping near that big island ahead. They're side by side like a raft."

"Maybe Kalabashar forced them to stop," Brandon suggested. "Why don't we fly closer."

At that instant a bright yellow object rose from the island. The object arched high into the sky, straightened out, and headed straight for the Responder.

"Missile!" Brandon screamed, ducking down.

Charlcie had no more than two seconds to flip the Oversight Lifter switch. The Responder plummeted hundreds of feet down, and the missile exploded in a huge fireball above their heads.

"That was close!" she shouted, shaking, searching below for any more deadly things. Two more screamed toward them and the Responder was barely able to avoid them.

"Take us down!" Matthew yelled when the noise of two more explosions had passed.

Charlcie steered the auto toward the eastern shore of the Red Sea. She flew it in a zigzag until she spotted a clearing in the barren mountains below. Quickly she guided the auto toward a safe-looking landing spot in the sand dunes.

"Any more missiles?" Brandon called from the floor where he huddled with Fongo.

"Not yet," Charlcie said shortly, occupied only with making a safe landing.

They bumped down with such force that Matthew and Mary were thrown forward. The Responder stopped almost immediately, up to its running boards in sand.

"That idiot caliph!" Brandon shouted as he sat upright. He glared at the island of Kalabashar, barely visible across the Red Sea. "We could have been an airliner with hundreds of people on board!"

"I'll bet all airplanes have been warned to stay out of this airspace," Charlcie said, removing her sweaty hands from the steering wheel. She breathed a long sigh of relief. "So much for your scouting expedition, Brandon. Now what?"

Brandon was still shaking. The most excitement he had had prior to this expedition was the time he fell out of a tree and broke his arm. He fumbled with his glasses, books, and maps, and tried to hold his compass steady. Then he moaned, sinking against the back seat. "I can't even think! Give me a minute. Then we should try to find some natives."

"I don't think we'll have to find them," Matthew said, gulping. Brandon opened his eyes. Matthew pointed behind the Responder.

Charlcie turned. Less than a hundred feet away on the sand dunes were some very ferocious-looking men. They wore robes, striped Arab scarves around their heads, and carried automatic rifles.

"Are those the natives you wanted to find?" Matthew whispered.

"Not exactly," Brandon whispered back as the men surrounded the Responder. It seemed, once again, that

75

their adventure would end abruptly. Then Brandon moaned, sliding down in his seat, "I don't want to die here! They'll bury us in the sand. The sun will bleach our bones!"

"What an imagination," Charlcie muttered. Then she called out, "Hello! Do any of you speak English?"

One of the men pushed his head scarf back. He rested his rifle against his shoulder and carefully approached the automobile. "Are you a witch?" he asked, shielding his eyes with his hand in case Charlcie gave him the evil eye.

"Yes!" Charlcie said flamboyantly as she stood upright with the red cape flowing from her shoulders. "And if you don't help us you will have plagues, droughts, and famines for six generations!"

All the men fell to the sand when their leader translated Charlcie's words. With his face on the sand, the leader begged, "Tell us what you want!"

"Come here!" Charlcie commanded.

Without hesitation the leader inched forward and bowed. He studiously avoided looking at Charlcie, but stared at the Responder in awe. "Your wish is my command, daughter of the sky."

"We've come from the sun," Charlcie said in her best vocal imitation of an actress she once saw in a movie about Cortez and the Indians. "With us we bring the power of wind and fire!" She whirled the red cape and it sparkled with fiery dust.

The men murmured and crouched lower on the sand.

"Say," Brandon asked suspiciously, "how come you speak English?"

The Arab leader shook his head as though awakening

76

from a trance. He asked Charlcie, "Who is this ill-mannered person?"

"A child of great learning!" Charlcie announced firmly.

"Ah," said the Arab, straightening. "I too am a person of learning. I have a B.A. degree from the University of Cairo in hydrology."

Brandon blinked. "What on earth is a student of waterflow doing out here in the desert?"

The man squared his shoulders and his bearded face almost became friendly. "I am with these Yemenite rebels at my master's bidding to help them locate springs and develop irrigation systems."

"And who is your master?" Charlcie asked in a regal tone.

The man bowed. "My master, O young mistress of wind and fire, is Caliph Kalabashar al-Khali, creator of the greatest rebirth of Islam since the seventh century, and commander of our Holy War against capitalism."

Charlcie was momentarily frightened by the man's words and his wild eyes, but she drew the red cape around her shoulders, stood on the seat, and said in her most queenly tone, "I wish to see this caliph of yours!"

Brandon and Matthew were terrified by Charlcie's words. Brandon managed to stammer, "That wasn't part of my plan!"

"It wasn't part of *your* plan," Charlcie hissed.

The Arab leader approached the Responder. He looked from the bewitched automobile to the young girl. She gazed back into his dark eyes with eyes as blue as oasis water. The Arab bowed again.

"I am Reyd al-Ayun. I will do as you wish." His

smile disappeared as he drew his scarf into place. "Come with me," he added in a deep voice.

"Quick," Charlcie whispered to her brother, "put the mice inside your shirt."

"Are you crazy?" Brandon demanded while Matthew hid the mice.

"Bring two of your biggest books and some water," Charlcie whispered to Brandon from behind her hand. She fixed her eyes on the rebels while the boys carried out her orders. Then, with all the dignity befitting a queen of wind and fire, she stepped out of the Responder.

Mary followed her. The girls linked hands as they walked across the hot sand toward the armed men.

"Will our automobile be safe here?" Charlcie asked the leader.

He pointed east toward a range of brown mountains which soared from the desert. His finger singled out the tallest mountain which was a towering hulk of broken rock. "That is Hadur Shuayb, Spirit Mountain. It will guard your vehicle."

"You will provide transportation to your master?" Charlcie asked.

The leader laughed. He sounded like a hungry bird of prey. "Your transportation will be what Allah provided, your feet." He noticed Mary was blind and frowned. "Who is she?" he asked with some apprehension.

"She is my guide," Charlcie answered calmly.

"Aiyee!" Reyd yelled, throwing up his arms. "How can a blind girl guide you?"

78

"She has many gifts from Allah," Charlcie said ominously.

Reyd cocked his head and studied Mary suspiciously. Mary let go of Charlcie's hand and walked straight toward Reyd. The other rebels stepped back, holding up hands to ward off evil. Reyd stood as still as a stone while Mary put her hand on the strap of the man's rifle and said, "You won't need this."

He jerked away, then waved his hands to make her blink. When he was satisfied that she could not see, he stammered, "Not even my master has such powers." Then he shut his mouth so hard that his teeth clicked. "Come," he said harshly, "my master will want to see you."

Mary took Charlcie's hand, Brandon followed, and Matthew trailed behind with Fongo who was miserable in the heat. The rebel band strode out in single file. They marched along the hard edges of scimitar-shaped sand dunes toward the sea, winding back and forth when necessary to avoid large pockets of soft sand. After more than two miles of climbing, they reached the crest of a hill. Below the hill was a village.

It lay at the edge of the sea. Its houses were built of sun-baked mud bricks. Their roofs were flat, some with brush canopies on them. In their yards were cone-shaped dove cotes of mud and small pens for sheep and goats. A few scrubby date palms promised little shade from the glaring sun. In the center of the village women in dark robes were gathered at troughs around a well. They were washing clothes and bathing children, but became motionless as the men led the children into the village.

Reyd pointed at some new houses. "That is where the doctor lives," he explained to Charlcie, "and that is where I live. Over there is the veterinary's home. Beyond it is where the school teacher lives. Before Kalabashar came, these people had no school, no doctor, no nothing. Now they have electricity, modern medicine, education, and food."

Brandon walked slowly, suspiciously, "You mean Kalabashar is helping these people?"

Reyd laughed and removed his face scarf as he approached the well. "What does it look like to you?" He accepted a goat-skin of water from a woman, washed his face and arms, then drank until satisfied. Then he sat at the edge of the well while the children drank. "Did you think the caliph was an evil man? That is what most Westerners think." He spat on the ground, then looked at the villagers who were watching the strangers.

"You said now these people have food each day," Brandon began, looking at the pleasant but watchful dark eyes that were staring at him. "Didn't they used to?"

"No," Reyd said emphatically. "They ate maybe three or four meals a week. No family ever had enough food. How could they obtain food?" He pointed at the barren countryside. "A little fishing, a few goats and their milk, some sheep, small gardens, and date palms only provided food—until Kalabashar came." He said loudly to the villagers, "Kalabashar." The watchers instantly responded with a cheer.

Reyd turned to the American children. "See how they feel about him? They worship the ground on which he walks. And they are not alone. Hundreds of thousands of poor people from many countries now look to Kalabashar for hope. He is freeing us from foreign domination. He is gaining fair prices for our only resource, oil. And he is making certain that the world does not treat our religion unfairly." He laughed. "Surely even you Westerners can understand their loyalty."

Charlcie looked at Brandon and Matthew. They were examining the villagers. The people did not look like slaves threatened by a madman. They looked content.

"What do you think?" Brandon whispered to Matthew and Charlcie.

Matthew seemed confused. Charlcie shrugged. "I have no idea what to believe," she whispered, "at least not about Kalabashar."

With that, she and the boys turned to stare at Reyd, wondering what manner of man his master truly was. Could it be that Kalabashar was not an evil man? Were General Throckmorton and other leaders of Western governments against Kalabasher just because he was trying to protect Arab oil and his religion? Were Professor Nesbit and other missing scientists not victims of kidnapping at all, but instead men who were volunteering to help poor desert people and their leader, Kalabashar?

Charlcie's jaw tightened. "We're ready to go to the island whenever you are," she said to Reyd. Mary squeezed her hand. The red cape was warm across Charlcie's shoulders.

7

Journey into Darkness

Reyd al-Ayun spoke to the rebels. They ran to the sea and untied a rowboat. Quickly they rowed out to a larger boat.

Brandon pointed at the large boat. "That's a dhow, a very ancient boat," he said. "The triangular sail they're letting down is a lanteen sail."

"I'm pleased to hear you know something about our way of life," Reyd said to Brandon. "Perhaps you will get to know us better during your stay."

Brandon studied the man, wishing people wore signs clearly indicating whether they were good or bad. Reyd watched the dhow bump against a stone jetty. As his men held the boat steady, the children and Fongo climbed into its low-sided waist and watched as the sail turned to catch a hot desert breeze. The boat tilted slightly and glided out onto the sea.

They sailed west until late in the afternoon. During the slow trip the children and Fongo found shade under the steersman's awning. The awning kept off the sun's powerful glare but did not keep the heat from baking them like pale potatoes in an oven. The mice and Fongo suffered most; often Matthew had to sneak drinks inside his shirt and splash water on the wolf's thick white fur to cool him.

By the time the sun had set, Matthew, Brandon, and Mary were drowsing. Suddenly Charlcie nudged them. She pointed ahead and they stared. The island of Kalabashar was clearly visible. Slowly its strip of sand dunes and low mountains grew larger. Nowhere on it was a sign of life. The dhow moved within a hundred yards of the shore.

Then it happened. Along the shore dozens of black things poked up through the sand like mechanical snakes. The black things were aimed at the boat and turned to track it as it sailed to the south end of the island.

"Laser cannons," Reyd explained with a smile. "Had we not radioed ahead while you slept, those cannons would have blasted us out of the water." He folded his arms. "Not even a bird can come closer than a half mile of the island of Kalabashar without the risk of being destroyed!"

Charlcie and Brandon cringed, wondering what kind of man Kalabashar was. What would happen, Brandon thought, if harmless fishermen strayed within range of the lasers?

The boat entered a small harbor. Its lanteen sail was lowered with a rattle, and two men jumped out into the shallow water. They held the boat steady while the children climbed out. Fongo jumped into the water, delighted with its coolness. He swam ashore last and didn't even shake the water from his fur as he followed the children and guards toward a bare hill a hundred yards inland.

As they walked the children looked for signs of a fortress or oil pumps. They saw nothing but sand, rocks, and low mountains until Reyd took a small transmitter from his robe. He pressed a button and within seconds the hill changed. A large door swung upward through the sand. From the black mouth of a tunnel came a squad of guards. Each was armed with a strange glass and metal weapon which Brandon assumed to be a laser rifle.

The guards from the tunnel talked with Reyd and his men. Occasionally they looked darkly at Charlcie and her companions and fingered their rifles. Brandon began to wonder if they were going to be shot. Even if the weather had not been blazingly hot, he would have been sweating rivers. He noticed, though, that neither Mary nor Charlcie seemed a bit concerned. For some reason their calmness made Brandon even more uneasy. He wished with all his might that he had never sneaked out of the window of his bedroom to join their expedition.

But it was too late for such thoughts. The new guards surrounded the children. They muttered commands in Arabic, which Reyd translated. "They say you must go with them." He pulled his face scarf over his mouth. "I have told them you are witches, so they will kill you the instant you make any suspicious movement!" He turned and led his men back to the dhow. Brandon watched Reyd leave with a feeling of regret; though the man seemed untrustworthy, he at least spoke English. Now Brandon wondered who would understand a word he or his friends said. What would happen to them if one of them had to go to the bathroom? That was precisely what Brandon wanted to do right now.

They were led by the silent guards into the dark mouth of the tunnel, and its door closed behind them with a frightening thud. Suddenly all was darkness, silence, and the chill of a strange, underground place. The children were uneasy. What was waiting for them in the darkness? Traps, dungeons, and torture rooms? Brandon and Matthew conjured up all the frightening possibilities and found themselves sweating even in the chilled air. But Charlcie and Mary still seemed unafraid. The boys hid their thoughts, held their heads high, and groped forward.

Walking in absolute darkness between armed guards was a disadvantage, however, only to children who were used to sight. Mary walked slowly but confidently forward, holding tightly onto Charlcie's hand. Charlcie reached back for Brandon's hand, and Brandon felt for Matthew's hand. Matthew led Fongo by an ear, something no one else would have attempted. Matthew felt increasingly uncomfortable; five nervous, thirsty, and half-suffocated mice were squirming under his shirt. He felt like screaming when one of the mice tried to scramble up his ribs with its scratchy claws but knew that if he screamed he would be blasted to charcoal by one of the guards.

On and on they went through the vast underground labyrinth. Cold air blew against the children's faces from side passages, chilling them even more. Occasionally the guards muttered in Arabic and barred the children's way with outstretched rifles. Whenever that happened, machinery began grinding as though heavy doors were being opened. Then the group would go on, farther into the darkness.

After more than an hour of walking they sensed a stone floor beneath their feet. Suddenly bright lights switched on. The children were dazed. Mary gasped.

"Who's there?" she whispered.

Charlcie held a hand over her eyes against the glare, and cautiously looked around. She saw they had entered a stone-walled room about twenty feet square. She also noticed the guards were leaving, pulling closed behind them a heavy steel door. Charlcie cried out, but it was too late. The door crashed shut. Charlcie had only seconds to see what was in the room before the lights went off. The only object in the room was a small television camera mounted on the ceiling. "No one's here," she whispered to Mary.

"Yes, someone is," Mary insisted. "I can feel it."

"It?" Brandon asked, trembling. "IT?"

"Yes, it," Mary said firmly. She moved cautiously around the room, feeling the walls with her fingers. "It's watching us."

"There's a TV camera in the middle of the ceiling," Charlcie said, looking up. She could see a tiny, glowing amber light which turned with a whisper of machinery to follow Mary's progress around the room.

"Whoever you are," Charlcie said in a queenly voice, "we mean you no harm. We've only come to see Professor Nesbit."

Silence.

"I know you're listening," Charlcie challenged. "Are you afraid of four children and a pet wolf?"

"I—am not afraid—of anything," a metallic voice

clicked. The voice seemed to come from nowhere, but Mary went immediately to the wall opposite the door.

"Who are you?" she asked softly.

"I speak for Kalabashar—most munificent of caliphs," the voice chanted. "I am the master—here."

"You sound like a computer," Brandon commented unhappily. He sat on the floor and wrapped his arms around his knees.

"You will be incinerated—in precisely four minutes," the voice continued.

"What?" Charlcie snapped. "Now wait just a cottonpickin' minute! Why did you bother to have us brought here if you were going to incinerate us? Why didn't the rebels shoot us first?"

"Three minutes," chanted the voice.

The boys scrambled up to search the room, tripping over each other and bumping into Fongo and the girls. But they found nothing. There was no way out.

"Two minutes."

"You're not Kalabashar," Mary said quietly, but firmly. "You may speak for Kalabashar but I'll bet he doesn't even know what you're doing."

Some hidden speakers hummed, then the computer voice said, "Upon what evidence do you base your conclusion—guide of the witch girl?"

"Kalabashar isn't a bad person. Incinerating four helpless children is something only a bad person would do," Mary replied.

The speakers hummed again, followed by a whirring-clicking sound. Then the metallic voice said, "One minute."

Charlcie grabbed Brandon and Matthew and made everyone join hands. "Pray!" she commanded.

This time the boys didn't hesitate. Matthew was already desperately mouthing his childhood prayers, but when he joined hands with the others, his prayers blended with theirs. "Lord Jesus," they prayed, "please save us. Don't let them kill us in this awful place. You're the only one who can help us now."

The minute was almost gone. Fongo whined, but the children kept on praying. The mice scratched inside Matthew's shirt, but he kept his eyes closed and his head bowed. There were only seconds left now.

Suddenly the metallic voice clicked on, screeching as if laughing. "I am testing your powers," the voice chanted. "I wished to determine if you truly were witches. You are not. Goodnight." The voice clicked off. The tiny amber light winked out.

"You dirty rotten garbage sniffer!" Brandon exploded. He jumped up and tried to hit the camera. "You lousy stinking transistor head!"

"Brandon?" Charlcie asked in amazement. "Is that really you talking like that?"

"That creep scared me!" he shouted, shaking his fist at the ceiling. Then he quieted himself, sighed, and sank to the floor. Charlcie even wondered if she heard him sniff.

There was silence for a long time. Everyone needed it to slow down racing heartbeats and shaky breathing. Only Mary was calm; she still seemed to be praying. Matthew spoke first. "Boy, Charlcie, this is some mess you got us into. You should've listened to Brandon."

"Yeah?" Charlcie replied hotly. "You didn't see those laser cannons that popped up from the beach?"

"Stop it please," Mary said firmly. "I'm trying to listen to something."

They sat in silence until Matthew and Brandon could stand it no longer. "What is it?" Brandon asked. "I don't hear a thing."

"I hear lots of things," Mary said. "I hear and feel people walking, machinery working, and something heavy being moved."

"Where's all that happening?" Brandon wondered, blinking.

"I'd say about three hundred-fifty feet away, northeast of us," Mary replied.

"You know where we are?" Matthew asked incredulously.

"Sure," Mary went on. "We came almost four hundred yards across the island and are now inside a mountain. To get out we'd have to turn left, go past six side-passages, turn right and go past fourteen cells like this one."

"Okay, I believe you," Matthew stated. "Whew! How'd you remember all that?"

Mary laughed. "Matthew, you forget. "We're in *my* world now. I am in darkness all the time."

Matthew rested on his back and opened his shirt. The mice were extremely happy to be free and were not at all troubled by the darkness. They scampered across the room to exercise their muscles and explore the room while Charlcie poured them a cup of water from Brandon's thermos.

"Ah," Padlock said with a sigh after his drink. "I was about smofficated!"

"Me too!" Whiskbroom agreed. The children heard her scratch her fur. "Matthew," she scolded, "you need to take a bath."

"Sorry," Matthew returned, rubbing his ribs where the mice had scratched him, "but I can't quite reach all of me with my tongue like a cat can."

"Say Padlock," Doorstop whispered, "I've found a hole."

"Yeah?" Padlock asked. "Where?"

"The steel door doesn't quite fit together," Doorstop answered.

Mary reached out to touch Whiskbroom and Padlock. "Please go out into the hall and turn right. Go about forty feet and turn left. Make a right as soon as you can and run until you see the entrance to a large workroom or laboratory. I'm sure guards will be posted there, so be *very* careful."

"Okay," Padlock gulped. "What are we looking for?"

"I think that's where the mechanical voice came from," Mary explained.

"Oh no," Padlock groaned.

"Be as quiet as you can," Mary cautioned.

While the mice scurried off to investigate, the children sat down to discuss things.

Charlcie began "What do you think of Kalabashar now?"

Mary touched her friend's arm. "The real question is—how do we get to Kalabashar?"

"You mean you want to see him?" Matthew asked incredulously.

"Yes," Mary said calmly. "That's why we came, isn't it?"

"No," Matthew answered roughly. "We came to rescue the professor."

"That's rather impossible," Brandon reminded his friend, "since we ourselves are in need of rescuing."

"The only person who can free us, or the professor, is Kalabashar," Mary stated firmly. "That's why we have to talk to him."

"Look," Charlcie exclaimed, "the cape is glowing."

Mary touched the cape's soft, warm cloth. "Something's going to happen," she decided.

"You mean it's warning us?" Brandon asked. He was sitting on his books, and suddenly thought it was strange for him to be trusting the instincts of a blind girl rather than the books he had always loved. But he could not deny the accuracy of her senses, nor could he ignore the fact that the cape was glowing with its own magic.

Before Mary could answer him, several things happened. First, Padlock and the other mice scrambled into the room. Breathlessly he reported, "Huge men, Dirk and Tirk, next to a tiny, horrible man in the workshop. The machine, our professor's big one, is being moved up into a dome-shaped thing. And, mean men are coming!"

Then suddenly the television light winked on. The light moved until it focused on the children. Then the metallic voice clicked on. "I have decided—that you are useless—to our operations. Therefore, you will be killed."

"Oh, you stupid creep!" Brandon shouted, grabbing

92

one of his heavy books. He hurled it upward, smashing the camera. Bits and pieces of plastic fell to the floor as the door began to open. The children stood flat against the wall beside the door. Fongo stood in the center of the room and began to growl. It was a deep, ferocious snarl which made the children's skin crawl with fear.

8

Escape?

A guard flicked a switch and the cell was bathed in white light. The guard saw Fongo facing him, and he instantly raised his laser rifle to fire.

Matthew leaped to knock the rifle away and kicked the guard in the shins as hard as he could. The guard yelled and fell to his knees as his rifle crashed to the floor. Three more guards rushed into the cell as Brandon snatched up the first guard's rifle. The guards tried to grab the children, but at that moment Fongo attacked.

He hurled his two hundred pounds into the air crashing into all three guards. They thrashed wildly about in their robes, screaming as Fongo's jaws snapped at them. Brandon, meanwhile, was quickly examining the laser rifle. "Ah-ha!" he cried, pressing a black button. A bolt of red light blasted out of the rifle's glass tip and burst into flames against the far wall of the cell. "Hm," Brandon smiled, "powerful thing." He aimed the rifle at the guards, but they were running like mad down the hall away from Fongo. Three more weapons were on the floor. Matthew picked one up.

Fongo was shaking his head; pieces of cloth and hair hung from his mouth. Matthew glanced at Charlcie. "Get a gun!" he shouted. "Let's blast our way out of here!"

"Don't be stupid," she said quietly as she reached for the light switch on the outside wall. Instantly, everything was dark again.

"What do you mean, don't be stupid?" Matthew hissed, going to her.

"Just that," his sister answered impatiently. "Come on, follow Mary."

"Follow her where?" Brandon wanted to know. "And why?"

"She told you why. We have to talk to Kalabashar. You two don't really believe we could fight our way out of here, do you?"

"No," Brandon said after a moment. He raised the laser rifle. "But it might be fun to try."

"Listen, you," Charlcie warned.

"Okay, okay," Brandon said, backing away. He tripped over his book, picked it up and stuffed it inside his shirt, then found his water bottle.

"Matthew," Charlcie continued, "let the mice ride in your shirt and hold my hand. Brandon, hold Matthew's hand."

"Aw, do I have to?" Brandon whined. "Couldn't we just shoot our way out?"

"No!" Charlcie said sharply. "Now come on!"

Matthew put his hands on the floor and the mice scampered up his arms to the inside of his shirt. Only Whiskbroom hesitated, whispering, "I wish you had found some time to wash."

"Meeow!" Matthew said, laughing as the little mouse jumped. "I can't very well take a bath in the middle of an escape." He waited for Brandon to take his hand.

"This isn't an escape yet," Mary stated from the hallway. When they were ready, she led Charlcie and the boys toward the workshop.

When they heard the heavy sound of marching boots, the children and Fongo ducked into a deep doorway. They held their breath until a company of guards went past them toward the cell they had just left. The children waited until the sound of shouted orders and thudding boots faded, then slipped back into the dark corridor.

Mary moved with painstaking slowness, each step bringing them closer to danger. They tried desperately to be quiet, but every breath they took and every move they made echoed loudly in the hall. By the time they reached the open doorway of the workshop the children's hearts were pounding so loudly they were certain anyone could hear them.

The workshop was lit up with powerful lights which were focused on a strange piece of machinery that was being hoisted into a dome. One side of the dome was an open slit like an observatory, and Brandon speculated the machine would be aimed out the slit once it was mounted. Charlcie took one look at the machine and whispered, "That's Professor Nesbit's Truthfall machine!"

Matthew peered into the lab and stared. "It sure is," he whispered back. "What on earth are they planning to use it for?"

Suddenly a metallic voice rasped out orders. It spoke

97

first in Arabic, then in English. "Professor Nesbit! Show the workers how to mount the focusing mechanism."

The children peeked around the edge of the doorway and saw—Professor Nesbit!

The old man made his way up scaffolding to a platform high above the concrete floor. He seemed very tired as he motioned to several workmen holding tools. He wore an open-necked white gown over which tumbled a mane of white, frothy-looking hair. His once rosy-cheeked face was gray now; dark circles of weariness framed the blue eyes which once had been bright with mirth and mischief.

"Be careful!" the metallic voice barked at the professor. "If you cause workers to damage the machine, your death will be infinitely painful."

Matthew and Brandon tensed, anger rising in their throats. Charlcie hushed them quickly. "Not yet!"

Matthew leaned around to see where the metallic voice was coming from. Brandon and Fongo leaned with him, safe in the darkness of the corridor.

On one side of the workshop was a kind of stage covered in purple cloth. The rear of the stage was lined with the blinking faces of several computers. Near the computers was a keyboard and control panel. Above this were more than a dozen television screens, each showing a different part of the fortress.

In front of the computers were two of the largest, meanest-looking men the boys had ever seen. Their huge beefy arms were folded over naked, hairy chests. Around their incredibly thick waists were broad black belts stuffed with pistols, knives, brass knuckles, and a curved sword.

98

Between these monsters sat a small, distorted figure. The metallic voice crackled from this ugly man. At his command an electric hoist attached to a steel beam at the top of the dome began to move. The Truthfall machine was raised higher toward the slotted ceiling.

"Those guards must be Dirk and Tirk," Matthew guessed, reaching into his shirt. He let Padlock take a look. The mouse nodded.

"Yep, that's them. Hear 'em laugh?"

Above the sound of clanging tools, the children heard a noise like bulls snorting. Tirk and Dirk were laughing.

"Do you suppose that awful little man is Kalabashar?" Brandon asked, looking at Padlock.

Padlock slowly shook his head. "That's not what the professor called him."

"It's not?" Matthew asked, surprised. He looked around the workshop as Padlock scooted back into his shirt. "Then who is he?"

Suddenly the professor leaned over the scaffolding to yell, "Yago!"

"It's *Master* Yago!" the little man screamed from his chrome and black-leather chair.

"Tell them to move the telescoping base under the machine," the professor called wearily.

Yago rasped out a series of orders. Workers ran to move a large, table-like thing under the machine. Slowly the legs of the base straightened to push up the Truthfall machine.

"Come on," Charlcie said suddenly. "Let's find Kalabashar."

The boys were reluctant to leave the professor, but followed Charlcie and Mary into the darkness. Fongo bared his teeth at the man on stage, then followed the children.

Down the endless passage they went, hand in hand, stepping carefully to avoid each other's heels. Brandon was amazed at Mary's sure-footed guidance. He was totally confused himself, until they came to a lighted intersection of several corridors. There Brandon noted by his compass that they were going north.

Later Brandon wondered why they hadn't met any soldiers. Wouldn't anyone who could make world governments tremble have soldiers? Finally he had to ask Mary. "Aren't there troops nearby?"

She stopped to answer him. "On both sides of this corridor I hear voices, thousands and thousands of them. Do you want to see who those voices belong to?"

"No," said the boy hastily, feeling cold sweat on his palms. "I just wondered."

But soon he too could hear voices. They sounded like the buzz of wasps in a nest. The sounds came from side passages and ventilator shafts. They made Brandon feel like he was walking through an anthill where insects might, at any time, attack. The buzzing became louder. Matthew's hand felt as sweaty as Brandon's. Brandon swallowed hard, wishing this was a dream he could awaken from at home, and in his own bed.

The buzzing separated into voices, and Mary stopped. Ahead, dim light defined the end of the tunnel. It opened into a great cavern, and from this place came the voices. Mary led her friends into the alcove.

"You three wait here," said Charlcie. "I'll go see what's ahead."

No one volunteered to go with her. Charlcie hadn't

gone far when she was stopped dead in her tracks by a loud, harsh voice. "You there, English girl! What you doing here?"

Matthew and Brandon trembled, but Charlcie seemed confident as she replied, "Taking a walk. What does it look like I'm doing?"

The voice softened. "You come back now to the harem. Kalabashar want you dance soon. You come quick; put on costume."

"All right," the other children heard Charlcie say, "but you'll have to show me the way. I'm lost."

Charlcie disappeared down the tunnel. Mary reached for the boys' hands and led them cautiously forward. What they saw at the end of the tunnel left them speechless.

They were standing at the edge of a vast cavern, nearly a half mile wide and high, which had been carved into the very heart of the island. In the center of the hall was a magnificent, white stone palace surrounded by terraces, pools, gardens, and lacy screens of carved stone. A weird kind of filtered light came through skylights cut from the cavern's roof. Brandon guessed the palace could easily house ten thousand people, but there seemed to be only a few thousand soldiers around the palace. It looked like the soldiers were impatient to be off on some mission.

Matthew grabbed Brandon's arm and pointed. Beneath them on a winding trail walked Charlcie. She had wrapped the red cape around herself up to her eyes, and behind her walked a tall, robed man who carried twin swords of gold metal. The man looked like a hawk, furious with having to retrieve a mere dancing girl. Matthew wondered where the real dancing girl was. What would happen if she showed up while Charlcie was in the palace? The boy was suddenly too anxious to watch anymore. He pulled on Mary's hand to make her go back to the alcove. There they waited, not knowing what might happen. Consideration of the possibilities made waiting almost unbearable for the boys. They would have run off screaming had it not been for Mary. She stood quietly, calm hands holding back the desperation of her companions.

Caliph Kalabashar al-Khali

Charlcie Arrow was very good at hiding her fear
behind a mask of bravery. But now her acting skills
were strained to the limit as she was forced to walk
past row after row of soldiers. She held her head high
and kept her eyes steady, pulling the red cape tight over
her Western-style clothes. The eyes of the hawk-man
bored into her back. If he even suspected Charlcie was
an imposter, she knew he would whack off her head
with his sword.

But he seemed to suspect nothing as they went into
the white stone palace. They walked past tiled pools
and gardens to the main building. Each room they entered was lavishly furnished; every floor carpeted with
lush, ornate Persian carpets. Every door was guarded
by enormous men who held their weapons as if they
wanted to use them. Charlcie held her breath until her
captor took her through the last door. Behind it she
could hear the high-pitched chatter of female voices.
When the door opened, she saw the harem of Caliph
Kalabashar al-Kahli.

About fifty beautiful young women were there, busy dressing in costumes and putting on make-up. Servants scurried here and there with wigs, flimsy dresses, and other crystal jars of perfume or make-up. In a nearby room musicians tuned instruments.

"Change!" her captor commanded, slamming the harem room door shut.

A servant approached Charlcie. She dressed the American girl in a silken costume, wound her hair into an elegant coiffure, and covered her face with sweet-smelling cosmetics. Charlcie felt like a doll. But she still had the red cape. She would rather have died than let go of the red cape.

A man entered the harem room and clapped his hands. The ladies' chatter ceased. The man in white shirt and white trousers spoke rapidly in Arabic and the women lined up. Then he singled out Charlcie and told her to stand at the head of the line. Charlcie wondered if he did that because the English girl she was impersonating was the caliph's favorite. Charlcie trembled, wondering what a fourteen-year-old girl could say to some filthy old man who kept a harem. She blushed despite all her efforts to hide emotion. The little man clapped his hands again and music sounded from an adjoining room. The line of girls moved forward.

The room they entered was grand. If Charlcie hadn't been so worried she would have gasped at its sheer beauty. At one end a fountain splashed into a clover-leaf shaped pool. Servants stood around the hall, each with his back to a gold column. Behind these columns floated gauzy white curtains. The ceiling was a high oblong dome of bright blue tiles twisting with delicate yellow tendrils. Exotic birds twittered in the bright air above a swirling, glittering mosaic.

The women stopped to form a semicircle facing a low platform opposite the fountain. There on a sea of pillows was a figure dressed in white, gold-trimmed robes. When he turned to the women, Charlcie gasped.

He was hardly a lecherous old man. Instead, he was a handsome young man about Charlcie's age. His dark eyes were not cruel at all, but instead so darkly peaceful that Charlcie doubted this was really the great caliph. The harem girls bowed, the musicians bowed, and the servants bowed. Charlcie bowed too, but not before the young man noticed her hesitation. Charlcie's heart skipped a beat. The young man smiled directly at her.

The smile melted Charlcie's heart and sent her suspicions fleeing. The smile was warm, tender, and unrestrained. It reached deep into her, compelling her to respond.

"Please come," the young man said. "Sit beside me while the others dance." When Charlcie hesitated several servants moved forward as though they would force her to the platform. But Charlcie gently moved on her own, feeling as if she was dreaming. Then she shook her head, reminding herself of the mission and the others who were waiting for her.

She curtsied to the young man, then seated herself. He touched a cushion closer to him and motioned for her to come there. She picked up the red cape and moved closer. Still the young man smiled. Charlcie stared at his face, then looked down, feeling her cheeks redden. She simply could not believe this young man would do anything evil, much less threaten the entire Western world with destruction!

The caliph clapped his hands. Instantly a weird, wailing sound rose from the musicians' instruments. The harem girls began to dance; whirling and swaying in time with the music. The young caliph leaned toward Charlcie.

"Who are you?" he inquired in perfect English.

Charlcie stiffened. "I'm the English girl."

"No," said Kalabashar, shaking his head. "Your auburn hair is more beautiful than hers. Your eyes are blue, hers were brown. I chose her myself so I know. Now who are you?"

Kalabashar's smile remained warm and friendly despite the questions, but his dark brown eyes examined her closely.

"My name is Charlcie Arrow," she said, swallowing with difficulty. "I'm an American."

"What are you doing in my domain?"

"Uh."

"Speak freely," he urged. "You are in no danger here if you speak the truth. However, if you lie—" He made a slashing motion across his throat with his finger.

Charlcie decided on the truth. "I've come to rescue Professor Nesbit."

The young caliph frowned. He rested his elbow on his knee, studying Charlcie. She returned his look without flinching. "Rescue?" he asked.

"Yes. Two of your men, Dirk and Tirk, kidnapped the professor from our home town. We, I've come to set him free."

Kalabashar looked puzzled. "Dirk and Tirk are Lord

Yago's body guards, not kidnappers, and we have no one named Nesbit here."

Charlcie looked into his eyes. "I've just seen him. He has been forced to set up his Truthfall machine in a domed workshop in the southern end of your fortress."

Kalabashar al-Khali sat up straight. Still looking into Charlcie's eyes, he slashed one arm through the air. The music and dancing stopped. The caliph waved again and the hall began to clear. Within two minutes Charlcie was alone with the caliph. Even the servants had gone.

He pressed his fingers against his forehead as if to push away pain, then frowned and looked down. "Please," he said in a low voice, "start at the beginning. Tell me every detail of your story."

Charlcie told him everything. Then she added, "Believe me, sire, sir, or whatever I'm supposed to call you, I don't think you're the kind of person who would threaten the professor, much less the world."

He was totally confused now. He stood up unsteadily. "I cannot believe what you've told me. You must be lying." He raised his hands to clap, but Charlcie moved quickly. She raised the red cape and whirled it over the young man's shoulders.

His hands paused as he stared at the glowing red cape. "What witchcraft is this?"

Charlcie smiled and sat down. "It's not witchcraft, sir. It's love."

Kalabashar laughed. "Love? No love can come from a cape!"

"Feel it."

He reached out suspiciously, then more willingly. Soon he was sitting on the cushions, stroking the cape's soft material. It glowed under his touch, lighting up his brown skin and dark eyes. His eyes softened as he murmured, "I don't know if it is love, but I like the way it feels. Is it magic?"

Charlcie nodded. "It's a special magic that belongs to Professor Nesbit."

"He made this cape?" the astonished caliph inquired.

"Oh, no," Charlcie replied. "It's very old, ancient as a matter of fact."

"It feels like the dew of early morning or like a dove's breast." He smiled again. "It feels like your lovely hair, only warmer." He reached to stroke her hair, then stopped at her cheek. "But not warmer than your skin," he said gently. Then he kissed her lightly.

She closed her eyes and returned the kiss. He sighed and sank back on the cushions. He put his hands behind his head and looked up at the birds flitting across the domed ceiling. "You are different from other girls who have been brought to me."

"I tell you truth, not just what you want to hear," said Charlcie quietly. She stroked the cape.

Kalabashar turned onto his right side and propped his head on his hand. "What should I do?"

Charlcie frowned, choosing her words carefully. "First, please explain how you had no knowledge of the things I told you. Aren't you trying to withhold Arab oil from industrialized nations? Aren't you organizing a holy war?"

Kalabashar closed his eyes and Charlcie stopped talking. He stared at the ceiling as he talked. "I am a special person, direct descendant of the prophet Mohammed. When the prophet died it was decided that

108

Muslims would worship Allah, not the prophet. However, descendants of Mohammed are specially honored. My father was a famous man, caliph of Baghdad in the days of Faisel II. When the revolution came to Iraq in 1958, my father lost his power. By the time I was born my father had come under the influence of Yago. He promised to restore my father and his family to prominence.

"Yago was a brilliant but impatient man, a scientist trained in the United States. Unfortunately he was grievously injured in a chemical fire. He is disfigured both in body and in spirit. He returned to the Arab world in 1960 and began working, as he said, to restore Arab states to their historical importance. He used my family name to give the movement credibility. Muslims will follow any descendant of the prophet, and I am now the only remaining heir of that name." He sighed as he rolled onto his side. He looked almost childlike now, and Charlcie felt a sudden urge to hold him.

"I was educated in Western ways," he resumed, "until my eleventh birthday. Since then I have been kept in seclusion. Yago, who understands politics and economics, has been my chief advisor since my father died. In fact, Yago is my only family because everyone else died of a mysterious disease which Yago says might kill me anytime I leave this palace." Kalabashar sounded miserable despite all his wealth and fantastic surroundings.

"What disease killed your family?" Charlcie asked.

Kalabashar shrugged. "The doctors say hereditary fever."

"Yago's doctors?"

"Why yes," the young man admitted. A strange thought made him frown. Then he stood and left the platform. "For years I believed him," he muttered. He paced to the center of the hall, then turned. "But for years I've wondered about what an old servant of mine whispered. He told me to beware of Yago's poison. I was frightened but had no idea of what to do." He knelt before Charlcie. "I ask you again. What would you have me do?"

Charlcie sighed. "I suggest you find out for yourself if what I've said is true. Only by believing in me can we help each other."

"Earlier you said we. To whom does we refer?"

"My brother, Matthew, my friends Brandon and Mary, and our pet wolf, Fongo, are waiting for me near the entrance of your cavern."

"Let's join them and confront Yago together," Kalabashar urged eagerly.

Charlcie frowned and reached up to take the hand he offered her. As she stood, she reached out to touch his lips with one forefinger. "If Yago has been in control all these years and is behind all the schemes I told you about, then if he's threatened you with a killer disease—"

"Oh," Kalabashar said, hesitating, "I see what you mean." He began to pace again, looking desperately around the chamber. "But surely the soldiers will side with me?"

"Who pays their wages?"

He stared at her. "Yago does, of course. But I am caliph! I am the religious leader!"

Charlcie looked at him skeptically.

"Ah," he muttered, "again I see what you mean." He walked a bit, then returned meekly to Charlcie. "I have never felt very strong. Now I feel extremely weak. How do you suggest we proceed?"

Charlcie smiled, taking both his hands in hers. "Perhaps," she suggested, "you are stronger than you know."

10

The Red Cape's Defeat

Kalabashar became very serious as he straightened to his full height. He removed the red cape, folding it carefully, and concealed it inside his gold-trimmed robe. Then he motioned for Charlcie to follow him.

Out of the chamber past guards and servants they walked. Kalabashar ignored the watchers until they began to climb the trail out of the palace cavern. There two guards blocked their path.

"Out of my way!" commanded the caliph in Arabic.

"But lord, Master Yago gave orders," one began hesitantly.

"*Master* Yago?" Kalabashar demanded in royal style. "Who is master here, you dog of the dunes?"

The guards fell to their knees and stretched their arms out before them. "You are, most munificent caliph."

Kalabashar and Charlcie took long steps past the prostrate guards and did not lessen their stride until they were in the dark tunnel leading south. Then Charlcie whispered, "Matthew? Brandon? Mary, where are you?"

Three children and one wolf slipped out of the shadows of the alcove. Kalabashar pulled back when the wolf sniffed at him but managed to smile at the children. "Greetings," he murmured, glancing uneasily at Fongo. Then he recovered his composure, straightened his robes, and held his head high. "Brandon, Matthew, are you armed?"

"Yes sir," the boys answered with surprise. Yet they obeyed him without question, holding up their laser rifles for inspection. Somehow the way Charlcie looked at the caliph assured the boys that the young man could be trusted implicitly.

"Good," Kalabashar stated. "I'll need you two to keep an eye on Dirk and Tirk while I speak with their *master*." His sarcasm was unmistakable. Charlcie wondered how many things Kalabashar had believed true were now agonizing suspicions in his mind. What did he believe now about the deaths of his family?

Through the twisting maze of tunnels they went. At first Kalabashar led, but when he became confused Mary quietly went first. She knew better than to shame the caliph in his own fortress. Besides, she was a person who received no pleasure in making others feel inadequate. When the young caliph got his bearings, she let him take the lead again. Soon they heard sounds of machinery and the shouts of workmen. Above all this was the harsh, metallic voice of Master Yago.

Kalabashar and his companions tiptoed through a side door. Then the caliph stationed Matthew and Brandon behind stacks of steel rods, whispering, "When I shout *duty*, you jump out and shoot Dirk and Tirk."

"Yes, sir," the boys replied stoutly, but despite all the

excitement of this adventure and the powerful feel of laser rifles in their hands, their stomachs were churning. What if they missed? What if the soldiers in the workshop opened fire? The boys were still asking themselves questions when Kalabashar walked toward the computer-lined stage where Yago sat.

"Greetings caliph," the metallic voice said in English. "I see that you disregarded my warnings."

"Yes, Lord Yago," Kalabashar said pleasantly. "I decided it is time I saw for myself the work you do that costs millions of dollars that might otherwise be spent on irrigation projects."

"The fever, my lord," the ugly little man warned. "It may kill you if you stay outside the palace."

Kalabashar smiled as he climbed the steps of the stage. "I will take that risk, Lord Yago."

The little man shrugged his shoulders. His jaw tightened and his eyes became hard. "What other risks have you suddenly decided to take?"

Kalabashar looked at Dirk and Tirk. The mountains of muscle put ham-like hands on their weapons. Kalabashar smiled with all the innocence he could manage. Though his heart began beating fast, he forced himself to turn his back on Yago and the guards while he examined the Truthfall machine. "I am curious. Please explain what this machine is for."

Before Yago could say anything, the white-haired old man on the scaffolding platform shouted, "It's a ray projector, young sir. Originally it was designed to reveal the inner motivation of man. Its penetrating light made liars glisten, cheats shine, and swindlers glow. But Yago has changed the function of this machine."

"Silence, heathen swine!" Yago shrieked, jumping up.

Kalabashar examined the little man deliberately, and all the workmen and soldiers turned to watch the stage. They were happy to see the young caliph away from his palace, for they knew that much went on without his knowledge. But they were afraid to side with him because Yago's temper was truly awful and his methods of torture were especially painful.

"What is the machine's purpose now?" the young caliph asked softly. One hand stroked the red cape inside his robe.

Yago cringed and managed a crooked smile. His yellow teeth gleamed between twisted lips. "It is reprogrammed to advance our religion, munificent caliph. With this machine's ray we can render the infidels powerless. No longer will they strip us of resources and pay us little. No longer will they threaten us with their foolish religion which claims their prophet arose from the dead while ours did not."

"Is it the will of Allah," demanded Kalabashar, "that you use this machine, missiles, and threats to advance our religion?"

Yago's eyes met Kalabashar's, and the young man almost cringed at the intense hatred he saw in them. Yago spoke deliberately. "It is Allah's will that we subdue an unjust and heathen world."

"It is your plan to begin *jihad,* a holy war?"

"Yes!" Yago spat.

"Even at the risk of losing millions of desert people I have tried to save from starvation and thirst?"

Yago's eyes burned with black fire. "Some must be lost in order that many may gain."

"How many gain, Yago? You?" Kalabashar asked.

"Yago raised his hand, and Dirk and Tirk hoisted their weapons.

"Tell your guards to wait, Yago," shouted Kalabashar. "They must do their *duty,* not what you wish!"

For an instant Kalabashar wondered if the boys had forgotten the code word. Surely he would have been shot dead had Dirk and Tirk not hesitated long enough to imitate their master's cruel smile.

But as they hesitated, Brandon and Matthew, gulping down fear, jumped into the workroom and leveled their laser rifles. As one they aimed at the stage. Workmen and soldiers dove out of the line of fire. Tirk and Dirk spotted the boys and tried to shoot, but bolts of ruby-red light lanced them. Laughter died on their lips as they fell, unconscious before they crashed to the floor.

As Matthew and Brandon fired, Kalabashar pulled out the red cape. He leaped onto the stage and before Yago could move, the young caliph whirled the cape around the little man's twisted shoulders.

"Aiyee!" Yago screamed, falling to the stage in a small pile of dark skin and bones.

"You're not hurt," Kalabashar said, fists on his hips as he stared down at the writhing figure.

"It *burns,* master!" Yago screamed, twisting back and forth. Matthew watched happily. Here at last was justice! "*Please,* young master, it burns!"

Matthew came with his friends to the edge of the stage. Suddenly he was touched by Yago's screams. Without wanting to, Matthew felt pity. He put his hands

117

over his ears to shut out Yago's cries and was about to ask Kalabashar to remove the cape. Then he saw the young caliph had other plans.

Kalabashar knelt beside Yago, putting his hand on the man's, narrow back. "If you lie very still, perhaps it will warm your stony heart instead of burning your body."

Yago stopped twisting. After a few minutes he began to smile. "Yes master, it is warming me."

"Good," said Kalabashar, patting the man on the back several times. Yago winced with each pat but did not protest. "Now," the caliph went on, "perhaps now we can do away with ray machines, missiles, and bombs?"

"Most certainly, young master," Yago murmured meekly, turning onto his side in a curled up position. He suddenly looked vulnerable, like a six-year-old child who had been in a fire.

Kalabashar faced the workmen and soldiers. "Are there prisoners and slaves in this fortress?"

Dark eyes turned toward the professor.

"Are there others?" Kalabashar asked.

A high-ranked official stepped forward. He clicked his heels together and bowed from the waist. "We have prisoners in many cells, my lord."

"Free them," Kalabashar commanded. "I want them taken to the mainland with enough money to compensate for all their time, efforts, and pain. Do it now!"

The officer motioned to the workmen and soldiers, who followed him out of the enormous laboratory.

Kalabashar turned to Professor Nesbit. "Do you wish to return home with your Truthfall machine?"

118

The old man carefully climbed down the scaffolding. Then he stood for several minutes looking up at the machine he had worked on for more than ten years. He turned to the young caliph. "May I do what I want to with it?"

Kalabashar nodded with a smile. "If it will do what you intended it for, it might change the entire course of world history. Yes, you may use it the way you want."

Matthew's head whirled. Just think! No longer could cheats, liars, and swindlers do their evil work in secret. Brandon speculated further. If the professor's machine could operate from a satellite so its ray would sweep over the whole world, then all evil would be exposed!

But during the time he had been forced to work for Yago, Professor Nesbit had changed his mind about the machine. He sighed, moving toward a small tractor. He climbed into it and started it up. Slowly he steered the tractor toward one of the telescoping legs supporting the Truthfall machine, and put a heavy wrench on the accelerator to keep it down. When the professor put the tractor in gear, it rattled forward. Charlcie and the boys gasped as the tractor crashed into the leg. The Truthfall machine tottered, then plunged toward the floor. The crash was deafening, and pieces flew everywhere. Fortunately no one was injured.

Charlcie and Matthew ran to the professor and hugged him. "I'm so glad you're safe!" Charlcie murmured, kissing his cheeks and smoothing back his mane of white hair.

"Me too!" Matthew said as Brandon joined them. "But why on earth did you smash the Truthfall machine?"

119

The professor looked at them sadly, but with a strange kind of content. "That machine," he said, "was the dream of an old man long angered by injustice even as you, Matthew and Brandon, are upset by things that are unfair." He looked at the scattered pieces of the machine and shook his head. "But who am I to say how others should be judged?"

Matthew's shoulders sagged. "I don't understand. Couldn't the machine have been used to expose evil people?"

"What would we have done to those people?" Professor Nesbit asked. "Have you ever told a lie? Suppose the machine exposed you, or Brandon? People might condemn you without offering you any chance to change."

Brandon blushed, remembering how he had slipped out of his home to come on this adventure. Matthew thought about when he had lied about Brandon's falling out of a tree and breaking his arm. Brandon hadn't just fallen. Matthew had pushed him.

Professor Nesbit smiled, guessing at the boys' thoughts. He looked at Kalabashar. "If you would, please return me now to my home." He laughed as he hugged Charlcie and the boys and Mary joined them. Kalabashar bent over Yago.

"Before I decide what to do with you," the young caliph said sternly, "answer me. What became of my family?"

Yago cringed under the cape like a beaten dog. "Truthfully, young master, your father died of natural causes. Your mother and sisters, though," He stopped and gagged. Speaking the truth was hard.

"Go on!" Kalabashar commanded.

Yago winced. "They are living unharmed, though in poverty, in Baghdad."

Kalabashar smiled. "So you have lied to me all these years?"

Yago cringed again, expecting to be kicked. "Yes lord, but, it was for your own good! Having a family clouds one's mind with emotions."

"Having a family clouds one's mind with love!" Kalabashar corrected. He frowned. "Perhaps you did not want anyone near me who would speak the truth? Or perhaps you wanted me to be as lonely as you feel." He looked at Yago with pity.

Yago was disturbed by the pity. "As you say, master," he mumbled.

"Yago," the young man whispered softly, "do you wish to continue wearing the professor's red cape?"

"No, young master," Yago muttered meekly. "If you would, please remove it so I may join those who are leaving the island."

Kalabashar hesitated, but then he remembered what the professor had said about the possibility of people changing for the better. Perhaps Yago too would change now that he felt the warming touch of love. Kalabashar lifted the cape.

Yago sprang up like a striking snake. Evil glittered in his eyes as he leaped toward the computer terminal. Before Kalabashar could stop him, Yago had punched a series of numbers on the keyboard. "Now," he screamed, "now we will all die! The Doomsoon bomb has been activated. Nothing you do will stop it! In precisely ten minutes, you and what your millions have bought will go up in smoke! I only wish I had stolen enough plutonium to make a bomb worthy of my hatred for this filthy world!" He shrieked with laughter which chilled the children to their bones. This, Charlcie Arrow thought, was truly the madman who had threatened the world. Then Dirk and Tirk began to move, struggling to join their master.

Kalabashar jumped off the stage and grabbed Charlcie's hand. The professor reached for Mary and they set off after the others at a dead run. The boys panicked, bumping into each other so hard that they dropped their rifles. Fongo crouched behind them as they struggled after the others, baring his fangs at Dirk and Tirk. The mad laughter of Yago pursued the children until they were a long way up the dark tunnel.

"Can we join the others who are escaping?" Charlcie panted as she ran.

"No," Kalabashar said. "Most likely they left in the supply boats hidden along the coastline."

"How can we escape?" Charlcie asked, barely avoiding a dark wall as Kalabashar slid around a corner.

"There's one hope," the young man said. "Run!"

Suddenly the red cape over Kalabashar's arm began to glow. Charlcie glanced at it as she ran alongside the handsome young caliph. She was thankful for what the cape had done to Yago, but wondered if the madman had actually been subdued. The last echo of his crazed laughter followed them as they raced down the dark tunnel.

11

The Doomsoon Bomb

Kalabashar and his companions sped at full speed down the endless corridor. Suddenly the caliph stopped to hit a glowing button on his left. A door slid open to a brightly-lit room. In the room stood a flimsy-looking rocketship pointing toward two steel doors. Kalabashar ran to the rocketship and opened a hatch. "Get in!" he yelled.

Everyone clambered in to find seats. Kalabashar went to the pilot's chair and frowned at the instrument panel. "Do you know how to fly this thing?" Charlcie asked, feeling panic.

"No," the young man admitted.

For an instant all hope seemed lost. Then the professor spoke. "Please, allow me. I watched Dirk operate the controls and I believe I can do the same." Kalabashar gladly turned over the controls to the professor.

The professor pushed down a switch, and the hangar doors groaned open to a long, straight tunnel. At the distant end of the tunnel was a tiny square of light.

Now the professor flipped some toggle switches and a whining sound came from the rear of the rocketship. Awful-smelling smoke began to fill the hangar, seeping into the aircraft's cabin. The aircraft strained forward. Suddenly the professor released a lever and the rocketship surged forward into the tunnel.

Dark walls flashed past as the square of light grew larger. From the rear of the ship Brandon called out, "Three minutes!" The roar of engines in the tunnel was terrifying.

Then light surrounded them as the rocketship soared into clear, blue sky. "Whoopee!" Matthew yelled, slapping Brandon on the back.

Brandon winced. "Two minutes."

As Professor Nesbit guided the rocketship over the island, everyone looked down at the Red Sea. Its sparkling blue surface was dotted with ships.

"Where to?" the professor asked.

Charlcie pointed east toward Hadur Shuayb. "The Responder is parked at the base of that mountain," she said.

The professor smiled as he aimed the rocketship toward the land. "So that's how you found me so quickly," he said proudly. "I always knew you were a resourceful young lady."

Charlcie grinned. Kalabashar looked at her with new appreciation.

"One minute until the Doomsoon bomb goes off," Brandon announced.

The professor nodded, guiding the rocketship toward the sand dunes beneath Hadur Shuayb. In a very short time the craft settled gently onto the sand. Everyone looked out the windows which faced the sea.

Fifty miles away a bright fireball burst. Upward the fireball rose, growing in size until it formed an enormous mushroom-shaped cloud. Within seconds blinding light flashed over the surrounding landscape. Then an explosion shook the rocketship, almost forcing it onto its side. Avalanches of rock crashed down the mountains, and a tidal wave rose from the sea toward the island of Kalabashar. As the children watched, the island simply disappeared.

The young people, Fongo, and the professor climbed out of the aircraft and stood on the sand, shakily facing the sea. Waves crashed against the shore. The mushroom cloud continued to boil upward.

"I hope all your people escaped," Charlcie said, reaching for Kalabashar's hand.

"Everyone but Yago and his henchmen," the young caliph said grimly.

"We're safe," Mary said with a shudder as she listened to the sea.

The professor put his arm around her shoulders. "Be thankful too that bomb wasn't a nuclear one."

They stood in silence for awhile. Then they walked around the rocketship to the Responder. The professor smiled as he patted its sleek fenders and narrow hood.

Meanwhile, Charlcie was talking quietly to Kalabashar. "I guess this is good-bye," Charlcie said sadly.

Kalabashar took her hands in his. "It doesn't have to be."

Charlcie looked into his dark eyes. "Today's Monday, I've got to get back to school."

"Come with me," said the young caliph. "I'll build another palace, and when we're old enough we can get married."

"What about your harem?" Charlcie asked teasingly.

"Oh, them," Kalabashar said, looking away. "They were just entertainment. Yago wouldn't let me have television or modern books."

"Is having a harem against your religion?" Charlcie asked.

"Yes, but marriage isn't."

She smiled. "What will you do, seriously?"

He looked north. "I'll fly the rocketship to Baghdad to find my mother and sisters. I'll stay with them until all the fuss settles down. Then, with the money from oil I still own, I'll continue to help poor desert people and city dwellers however I can."

"You won't try to strangle Western nations by withholding oil or selling it at outrageous prices?"

He shook his head. "Please do not leave believing all Arabs are like Yago. I promise you greed will never dwell in my heart."

Charlcie patted the red cape. "Love is better in the heart, isn't it?"

He smiled and stroked the red cape. "I'd like to keep this. Do you think the professor would sell it?"

"I can give you something that offers a lot more love than the cape," Charlcie replied.

"What?" Kalabashar asked, handing her the cape.

Charlcie reached inside her blouse and pulled out a gold chain. On the chain hung a small, golden cross. She offered the cross to Kalabashar. For a moment he hesitated. His face looked tortured. Then he looked into

Charlcie's confident, bright eyes and bowed his head. She pulled the chain over his glossy black hair and placed the cross against his chest. Gently they kissed. Then they said good-bye.

Kalabashar waved to the boys and professor, then walked back to the rocketship. The professor started up the Responder while Matthew shook the mice from his shirt and turned them loose in the back seat. Brandon offered them water from his thermos bottle. With tears in her eyes Charlcie climbed into the automobile. She had the feeling that someday she would see Kalabashar again.

Professor Nesbit pressed the accelerator. Quickly the Responder rose from the sand and soared into the sky. It banked near the cliffs of Hadur Shuayb and turned west. Charlcie Arrow wrapped herself in the red cape and went to sleep. The other children also dozed, and even the mice sacked out, nestled in Fongo's fur. They all slept so peacefully that they didn't see the mushroom cloud pass beside them, Africa fade beneath them, or even the Atlantic Ocean's gray vastness.

In fact the children didn't wake up until the professor called out, "Want to see Washington, D.C.?" The wind lifted his mane of white hair as he leaned over to look down at the capital.

The children yawned. "We've seen it," Matthew said. Then he sat up, rubbing his eyes. "Remember Robert Downing and his offer?"

"What offer?" the professor inquired, turning.

"A reporter from NBC offered us a half million dollars for exclusive rights to our story if we succeeded,"

Brandon said happily. "And I believe we have succeeded."

"Not exactly by ourselves," Mary cautioned, stroking the red cape which Charlcie had been sharing with her.

This time as the Responder landed at Dulles International, no Air Force jets shrieked overhead and no emergency vehicles raced out. Security police also were missing, however, a curious crowd did gather at the huge, gray windows of the terminal. While the professor went inside to call General Throckmorton, the crowd stared at the Responder. The young people in it smiled and waved.

After a long time, Charlcie saw a tall man with brown curly hair and a television crew work their way through the crowd. "There's Robert Downing," she said to the boys.

They climbed out of the Responder to meet the reporter and shook his hand while the cameraman caught everything on film.

Matthew could hardly wait to ask. "When do we get our half million dollars?"

Mr. Downing frowned, signaling for the cameraman to stop filming. "Um, there seems to be a problem with that."

"What?" Brandon demanded, pushing up his glasses decisively.

"For one thing," the reporter explained, "the offer has been withdrawn."

"Why?" Brandon whined, stamping his foot. "You mean you're welching on the deal?"

"No," Robert Downing said slowly, "but it seems you didn't succeed."

"Oh, yes we did!" Brandon and Matthew shouted.

Mr. Downing shrugged. "The Central Intelligence Agency released a report this morning that their agents had successfully blown up the island and its madman, Kalabashar."

The boys stared speechlessly. Brandon wished he hadn't left his laser rifle in the workshop. Then Matthew finally sputtered, "But Kalabashar wasn't the bad guy. Kalabashar is a young caliph who was used by a crazy scientist named Yago! It was Yago who blew up the island with his Doomsoon bomb!"

Mr. Downing laughed gently. "I'm sorry, but that's a pretty incredible story. Besides that, no one will believe you because the CIA has released their version of what happened."

"That's not fair!" Matthew shouted, then choked. His face turned red. Slowly he turned toward Charlcie. She was sitting in the Responder, laughing. "Oh, be quiet!" he snapped.

Mr. Downing cleared his throat. "It may not be fair, but that's the way things are. The CIA couldn't admit four kids did what their agents failed to do, could they?"

"No," Matthew admitted, hanging his head. Then he raised his eyes to look at Brandon, Charlcie, and Mary. "But *we* know what really happened, don't we?"

The four young people began to laugh. They were still laughing when the professor returned.

He glanced at the reporter and spoke quietly to the children. "I got in touch with General Throckmorton," he said. "Strangely, the general didn't seem disappointed that the Truthfall machine had been destroyed. He told me that a great many people in Washington had begun to oppose the whole idea of such a machine." He chuckled as he slid onto the driver's seat. "I suppose everything works out for the best."

"Can we film your take-off?" Robert Downing asked. "It'll make the six o'clock news nationwide and make you famous."

"Keep your fame," Matthew huffed. "You can film all you want to. It's still a free country—and a free world, you know."

Robert Downing frowned as he watched the bright red automobile take off. And he never did figure out why the young people and the professor were laughing.

By sunset the 1924 Responder was flying over their home town. Charlcie and the boys leaned out eagerly. It seemed they had been away an awfully long time. They could hardly wait to see their families and friends.

"Before we land," the professor said, "I want to thank each of you for what you've done. Never have I seen such bravery and sheer persistence!" The young people grinned. Even Fongo and the mice seemed happy. Charlcie noticed that the professor's eyes once again had their merry, bright blue sparkle as he winked at her and patted Mary lovingly on her head.

When the boys looked down again, they spotted Professor Nesbit's vine-covered cottage. Several cars were parked in front of it. The professor deftly guided the Responder over the cottage and landed the car gently. It rolled up a hill and into the open barn.

Charlcie and Matthew got out first and began unloading the suitcases. Then they heard a familiar voice.

They turned to see their father, waving to them as he entered the barn. They flew into his arms.

"Dad!" the children shouted. "You came back!"

"Yes," he said, kissing them several times. "I got a frantic and not too understandable phone call from Mirabelle, so I decided I'd better fly home. I arrived in time to watch the evening news and a film clip of you taking off from Dulles International." He hugged them. "You're quite a bunch of heroes for bringing Professor Nesbit home."

"Dad, that's not the half of it!" Matthew whooped. He and Charlcie started their story while their father sat on a running board of the Responder. He was so fascinated by what he heard that he barely noticed five mice leave the automobile. They were welcomed by a squealing crowd of their friends—though the cheering of the mice was so quiet that only Fongo and Mary heard it. Fongo sat by Mr. Arrow and affectionately bathed his hands while the Arrow children took turns telling all about their adventure.

Meanwhile, Brandon was lugging his suitcase toward the barn doors when he saw his parents. He ducked his head, expecting to be punished. But his parents were so proud of him that the only punishment he got was losing the book he d thrown at the television camera. Later his mother bought him all the ice cream he could eat.

Nearby, Mary Bradley's parents, too, were so thankful to find her safe that they forgot all about her missing camp. In fact, when she told them how the adventure had succeeded, they were certain it had been better for her than camp.

The next person to come into the barn was Mrs. Nesbit. She and the professor embraced for a long moment, then slowly walked down the hill toward their cottage. Then suddenly Professor Nesbit looked back. "Charlcie," he called, "please keep the red cape for me." She hugged it tightly as he smiled and disappeared into a group of people rushing up the hill.

They were reporters eager to get the Arrow children's story. But in front of them raced a bustling, flustered looking woman. She stopped in front of Charlcie and Matthew and put her fists on her hips.

Charlcie grinned. "Mirabelle, aren't you glad to see us?"

The housekeeper flashed a broad smile. "Yes!" she exclaimed.

Charlcie and Matthew rushed forward to kiss her. Then they all left the barn. As they walked down the hill they ignored the clamoring reporters and talked about the homecoming meal Mirabelle had prepared. Then Charlcie and Matthew dropped back to walk beside Fongo, who was being carefully avoided by the reporters.

Charlcie folded the magic red cape over one arm and patted it. Then she whispered to Matthew, "Next time we'll know where to find this when we need it!"